"I made it home all right that night, head full of strange angles, Claire, the smell of her still fresh in my melting brain, an intense and beautiful throbbing at the back of my head–The next day I wrote *Snakes*. . . . The title sounded weird to some of the people we knew but the title was very important. The idea for it had come to me from a number of places but most notably from the expression *fattening frogs for snakes* that I'd heard Jezzy and Claude use a thousand times. Also, the melody itself was made up of tricky lines that to me sounded snake-like. The tune sounded simple the first time you heard it but it wasn't all that simple to play. . . . I was in my glory up there on the stand, not quite like in the dream but doing all right; cool. . ."

This is the story of MC: young, black, and his head full of music. Orphaned at an early age, he lives with his hardworking grandmother, Claude, who plays the numbers with the same passion that he plays his electric guitar. He, with his drummer friend Shakes (short for Shakespeare) form a band; turn on to new sounds with another friend, Champ; play the school gigs, parties, TV talent show; and cut the record *Snakes* which becomes a local smash hit. There is a heavy scene with drugs and hassles, and MC splits to New York alone. This novel is written with the rhythms and nuances of a delicate musical score.

AL YOUNG began singing and playing blues in Detroit. He also wrote prose poetry, worked as a disc jockey and edited humor journals; some of his work was published in little magazines. After graduating from Berkeley, he won a Wallace Stegner Writing Fellowship and a National Arts Council prize. He now teaches as Jones Lecturer in Creative Writing at Stanford University.

SNAKES

A Novel by

AL YOUNG

Published by
Dell Publishing Co., Inc.
750 Third Avenue
New York, New York 10017

Laurel ® TM 674623, Dell Publishing Co., Inc.
Reprinted by arrangement with
Holt, Rinehart and Winston, Inc.,
New York, New York
Printed in the United States of America
First Laurel Edition—February 1972

Much of this book was written on a
Wallace E. Stegner Fellowship, an honor
and aid of which the author is deeply
sensible. Sections of it, in slightly
different form, appeared in *Nexus: The
San Francisco Literary Magazine*.

For my mother, my father, my sister
& brothers; for the family, in memory
of Mr. Simmons, & for Arl

. . . music, being such a medium as it is, can affect you all your life. Music is not only a God-given talent, it is a God-given privilege to play music. There shouldn't be any debauchery attached to it. It should be presented in the exact spiritual vein originally intended. It is something within ourselves.

—Jo Jones
Hear Me Talkin' to Ya

I sent for Padio, my trombone-playing friend who lived in Oakland. (Poor Padio, he's dead now, never got East so none of the critics never heard of him but that boy, if he heard a tune, would just start making all kind of snakes around it nobody ever heard before.)

—Jelly Roll Morton
Mister Jelly Roll

Talking with one another is loving one another.

—Kenyan Proverb

SNAKES

PART ONE

ONE

Most of my life Ive been confused. Very little that I hear or see going on around me makes any sense. I don't always understand what people are doing. I take them on faith and play things by ear which means that Ive been let down a lot. But one of the few things that's never let me down is music—not musicians, not promoters, certainly not club owners, recording companies, critics or reviewers—Music!

I listen and look for it everywhere I go: in the streets, in the country, in people's voices, in their movements, in the way they lead their lives. There are pictures and scenes that sing to me; the right words can set my head to vibrating with music; certain women arent melodies to me but lovable fields of musical energy.

I had a record going for me once when I was a kid, before I knew very much about music; a modest success, a single called *Snakes* that caught on for a few weeks in my hometown. Up until then I had vaguely thought I wanted to be one of the boys, something other than what I was at least. I had been expecting some big magic moment to tick off at which time things would fall into place and everything about me would be transformed.

Well, MC, I said to myself, here's your chance to show the world what you can do; all those ideas youve been building, all those dreams, all those feelings—now theyre waiting to drop whatever theyre doing and listen to what youve got to say, and when they hear, when they finally and truly hear you, how can they not help but say: This man's got Soul, and a beautiful Soul at that.

That's the trip that I was on.

TWO

PANCHO, my own true daddy, was a musician, it's said, a singer, but I never got to hear him. I never saw him nor my mother Flo except in old photographs, old snapshots in albums that my grandmother kept. It was Claude, my grandmother, with the help of her common-law husband Bo who died when I was ten, who raised me and encouraged me to take on the world, and I love them every bit as if theyd been my mother and father.

I always think of the picture of Pancho in the fading photo where he's posed by himself: he is as sharp as the times will permit, smiling suavely, sporting one of those hand-painted ties, coat open, hair trimmed short, pomaded and slicked back; a large brownskin man with a thick Genghis Khan mustache—and the eyes, the eyes are for real and forceful, large dark eyes that say to me: "I am only a young man but life is not unknown to me, and although I'm posing momentarily for this formal photograph, I do live as fully as I'm able during my informal unphotographed hours. I am a very hard-working man who loves the girls." That "loves-the-girls" look shines not only from his eyes but from his whole face which bears witness to the fact that he's also something of a rascal.

In another photo—the one where he and Flo, my mother, are posed together, mugging for the camera in front of everyone at some big class picnic that took place on Belle Isle back before I'd come to Earth—he's got on one of those old floppy slouch hats worn by film detectives of the 1940s and a dark V-neck sweater revealing a triangle of plaid cotton shirt. He's barefoot, standing in the sand, grimacing, about to chomp down into a big Dagwood sandwich. Flo's right there beside him, cheering him on, egged on by all the other classmates. He's got hold of her and she too is wearing a simple sweater, plaid skirt; her hair is straightened and piled up on her head; she's smiling, black-eyed, twinkly, a bobby-soxer sure enough. I can even make out the water itself way in the almost no-background of the murky Detroit River. Everything is black and gray.

In another picture, actually the only other Pancho picture I know of, he's out on the sidewalk in front of what must have been the house where he lived with his family. His feet are slightly apart. He's taken his coat off, the same one he's wearing in the original shot, and has it draped over one arm. With his free hand he's waving at somebody in the foreground. His shirt's open at the throat and there's a small crucifix hung around his neck. It must be a very bright afternoon because he's squinting, and a little lighter in complexion than he is in any of the other shots.

When I was little, I used to like to imagine that he was waving directly out at me from that picture, saying, "Goodbye, MC, goodbye. I'll be back one of these days but I got to go now. Take care of yourself and dont let anything get you down."

When I asked Claude what the crucifix was all about, she said, "O, old Pancho like to wear that thing around sometime, not all the time, just when he was in a certain mood, Sundays mostly, after church. He sung up here at some little church and use to all the time be talkin bout how he was gon get up a gospel group and make a record. I use to get after him not to be wearin that necklace cause I thought it looked kinda sissyish, but I dont think your mother minded it all that much. I always figgered she'd probly done seen some man had one on in the picture show or someplace and thought it was cute."

Claude was history, my one close blood connection with the past. She had run away from home in Mississippi at fifteen with a man almost old enough to be her father. She had gotten pregnant by him and he had deserted her in New Orleans. Finding herself a long way from home, a long way from the farm, the mules, and Mama and Papa and something to eat, she wandered the city and found work in a honkytonk where she met Bo.

"Child, lemme tell you, they like to work my tongue palate out! Had me waitin on tables and doin a little some of everything. It was a nigger come in there one night was smokin cigars and keepin up a whole lotta racket kept cuttin his old bloodshot eyes at me. He was in his glory cause he was winnin at the crap tables in the backroom and after reckly he'd done taken everybody's money, so he commence to grinnin all up in my face and tryna buy me drinks. Drinkin was somethin I wasnt too use to in them days. Bout the strongest thing I'd ever got hold to was co-cola. He found out from the fella that run the place that I was new around there and didnt really have no place to stay, so that cigar-smokin Negro insisted I stay at his mama's place, told me his mama run a roomin house a little ways out from there and if I was innerested he'd be glad to carry me over there hisself after I got off work. Well, I said, all right, I'd drive on over with him and take a look at the place. But the way it turned out, the nigger did drive me someplace all right but it wasnt to no roomin house. He had a pint in the car and wanted to try to get me drunk so he could show out on me, but I'd done already got sicka one man usin me like that, the one I run off from home with, so I got this rascal told right quick. He got hot about it, told me I didnt preciate a joke. I just set there and looked at him like he was crazy, which he was. He finally cooled down and got real nice, you know, and said he was sorry. I asked him would he please mind puttin his old nasty cigar out cause the smoke was making me cry when the real reason I was cryin was I was scared I'd gone and done the wrong thing—gone and got myself into all that mess. I broke down, child, and cried like a baby, and I guess the nigger got to feelin some kinda sorry for me cause he told me I could stay at his place that night if I didnt have no place else to go, said he wouldnt bother me none. 'Dont be scared of me, baby, I aint no rattlesnake!' For some reason, I taken him for his word and went with him to his place which wasnt bad considerin he wasnt much more than a little nickel and dime crapshooter and cardplayer. He slept down on the floor that night and let me sleep up in the bed. I remember it was a big rain come up and he got up offa his pallet and taken a blanket and covered me up with it. He said I could stay there long as I felt like, said he'd done won enough money gamblin to go upnorth and get a good job in a factory. I ended up comin north with him on the train to Detroit. Little after we got here I found out I was pregnant by that man I'd run off from home with but I was scared to tell Bo. He'd been so nice to me. But he found out finally and told me it was all right with him if I wanted to go head on and have the baby, that he'd help out the best he could. We worried bout it a little bit but we'd done got to kinda like one another and I went for the man, seein as how he was really so gentle and kind underneath all that bad talk and bad livin he'd been doin. I'm not that proud about it but that's how your mother come into the world. I named her Flo because I always did think that was such a pretty name for a little girl."

I could listen to Claude talk all day long, and did, many a time. Her voice was like music.

She and Bo were the only mother and father I ever knew. Pancho had been trying to support Flo and his mother and brothers and sisters too. The strain of it must have become too great for him because finally he quit his job at Ford's and disappeared. No one knew where he was. Then one day Flo got a letter from him saying he was in Chicago and wanted her to come see him. He even sent her a one-way ticket. She took the train to Chicago, leaving me behind for Claude to take care of.

"She stayed over there and stayed over there," says Claude, "which was messin me up cause it was wartime and I was pullin a shift myself out here at a plant and was usin up all my sick time to stay out and look after you. By Flo stayin over there so long my boss was gettin suspicious. After while she and Pancho called up long distance and told me theyd done talked it over and made up they minds they was gon stay on together and was comin back here to Detroit to get married. They was gon drive back in some old piece of car Pancho'd done picked up, a old Chevy. Anyway, they got back here to Michigan thru all that snow and ice and sleet and mess—I remember it was pretty cold, done got down to bout five or six degrees above zero cause all the pipes froze up over there in the projects where we was livin—so they got out here round Ypsilanti where Flo got out to call me up and say we could look to see them in a hour or two. I thanked God theyd done got back all right cause all you heard over the radio was how slippery and bad the roads was.

"So after that they musta drove on long a good piece before they car skidded into a truck, or either the truck skidded into them. Didnt nobody ever find out how it went, least not to my satisfaction. Flo was killed instant. She died outright. But Pancho was still alive when they got him over to the hospital—even tho it look like to me they taken they own sweet time gettin him there, on accounta it was one of us, you know, on accounta it was colored. By the time they got him out the ambulance on into the emergency, he'd done passed, say he bled to death. When I heard tell of it—the police and all of em come out to the house to let us know—I went into a decline for the longest and was laid up low sick. Bo told me, 'I guess God must know what He doin, hunh?' I asked him how come he come askin me somethin like that. He say, 'Cause I sure in the hell dont know what He doin.' "

When I think of Claude, I see a slim dark-skinned woman in a cotton dress or some old skirt and baggy sweater. She's seated at the kitchen table by the telephone fingering a dreambook or a paperback mystery. She loves detective books. She's sniffing her coffee ("Dont drink it," she'd tell me, "itll make you blacker than you are already!") and is about to light up a Camel cigarette poised between the smoking fingers of her left hand which are darker than all the others. Her hair is pressed and brittle, held by a headrag tied tightly at the front. Her eyes are large and droop. Theyre unusually brown; brown pupils flecked with brown. She's all brown: I see her feet on the floor in raggedy house slippers, legs spread quite thoughtlessly, enough for me to peek at the tops of her stockings beginning their roll just above the grayish knees. She's young for a grandmother, having had Flo at sixteen, and is flattered anytime anyone tells her so.

She's the last person in the world I would want to hurt.

THREE

FINALLY I keep trying to see myself emerging out of that shaky home scene, a home-grown nut, a peculiar lad who lived with his hard-working grandmother who spent all her extra money playing the numbers and playing them hard. She always wanted to hit lucky and ease out of the game, all the games.

When I was ten, Bo died and Claude took sick and didnt have the means or strength to look after me properly, so I was sent south to live with relatives. They were cousins but I called them Uncle

Donald and Aunt Didi. They lived in a small town in Mississippi and were poor as church mice the first year I spent with them. We lived in a rickety old frame house out from Meridian and had neck-bones, rice, or beans and rice for dinner a lot. Uncle Donald sold fruits and vegetables on the streets from an obsolescent truck and in summer was the original watermelon man.

Uncle Donald was also what they called a mid-night rambler who drove Aunt Didi into fits. He liked to stay out late. The ruckus he kept up was continuous. He got into fights. Wherever he went there was commotion. But he had a talent for get-ting hold of a dollar and dollars were very scarce indeed.

He bought an old used humpback Ford and had the legend BLACKJACK TAXI CO. stenciled on the sides and drove around town picking up fares. Soon he had the good fortune to acquire three or four other cabs. Business was good, but there was only so much money to be made off black people who took taxis in a small southern town.

Uncle Donald started running whiskey for a black bootlegger who, allegedly, was being backed by a white man whom some people identified as being the governor himself. Within a year after I had come to live with them, quickly adjusting to the southern style of life and the funnytime pub-lic school system, Uncle Donald turned the house into a beer garden, a blind pig where people slipped to have a few drinks, gamble, dance, or just generally cut up and get their feet wet in the dry, dry state of Mississippi. The sheriff himself was often to be seen on the premises, a black gal on either arm, loaded to the jowls and red in the face, quivering when he put on his big white horse-laugh.

My second cousins and I, Aunt Didi's and Uncle Donald's children, were all around the same age. Their oldest boy, Jab, was exactly my age. We thought it was great that there was a party going on all the time. We were regularly called in after the sun went down and playtime was over, and hustled into a back bedroom from which we'd work our game of listening thru the walls, making numberless trips to the bathroom in order to get a peek at all the people and see what all the fuss was about that went on and on into the night.

Records would be playing, drinks poured; women and girls laughing and cackling in high black tones and registers. I used to sit with my cousin Jab by the wall next to the door and read comicbooks and dig all the sounds seeping thru. We'd split a pack of B-C Headache Powder, dump it into our palms and lap it up with a Coke or RC. We'd seen grown people down south doing that. We knew all the records by heart, all that blues and rhythm and blues, those jump numbers and jazz, even country and western sides, cracker music. "Wouldnt you like to be able to sing or play somethin when you grow up?" I asked Jab.

"Like what?"

"Like anything—just be able to make all that good sound come outta somethin and get paid a lotta money for it."

"How much money you think people that put out records get?"

"I dont know but I know it's a lot."

"A thousand dollars?"

"I dont know. A thousand maybe, five thousand, maybe even ten thousand. They get a lot all right."

"How you know?"

"Well, it's a lotta people buy they records, you know that."

"How many?"

"Look at how many records Uncle Donald and them buy—and that's just around here. Think about all over the state and all over the country and the world and everywhere."

"You think they get as much as a boxer?" Jab was hung up on becoming a prizefighter.

"Some of em do, I betcha that. I betcha it's a lotsa boxers dont make as much money as some of these people put out records."

"How much you wanna bet?"

"Bet a dime."

"Where you gon get a dime from?"

"I'll get it, dont worry bout that. You wanna bet or not?"

We worked up a routine for hustling drunk people on their way into or out of the bathroom. We knew how to get them into conversations that ended up with them shelling out a nickel, a dime, or sometimes even quarters. Whenever we managed to con someone—usually a half-high older man in a jolly mood—we'd get back into the room and dance and brag about how slick we thought we were.

The music, I noticed, seemed to make people happy. At least it made things seem more relaxed and pleasant. It was the music that was knocking me out. I thought about songs and listened to everything. When we went to church—one of those churches with a band full of trombones, trumpets, saxophones, piano, organ, tambourines, the works—I yawned and dozed thru the draggy sermons and more proper singing, knowing that things would get better as the meeting warmed up. As soon as the spirit would begin to hit, the band would let itself go and blast away, ladies fainting, me sitting there, sometimes trembling with fright but loving every minute of it; other times so quiet and caught up in the excitement that Aunt Didi would have to look around to see if I was still there.

Uncle Donald worked some kind of deal that resulted in an old beat-up upright with a couple of missing notes being hauled into the front room for the pleasure of piano-playing customers who got the urge. It was a rough-looking instrument, battered, many of the keys yellowed or chipped, but it had been newly tuned and had a curious oldtime sound that I found attractive. It must have gotten several years' worth of wear the first few months it was with us. House guests played away at it evenings and midnights, and during the day we kids banged at it, hunt and peck, diligently fashioning right- or lefthand versions of whatever tunes suited our fancy.

I learned that I wasnt bad at it and, before long, could rattle off just about any melody that struck my ear and from any number of starting points on the keyboard. Aunt Didi wanted me to take piano lessons but I thought that was too sissified and told her I wasnt interested.

Eventually my chance to learn a few things came up anyway. A thin man with a limp came in one afternoon in the summertime to take care of some business with Uncle Donald. It was very hot outdoors so a few of us were lolling around the kitchen drinking Kool-Aid and enjoying the electric breeze from the fan Uncle Donald had bought hot. Business transacted, the thin man sat down at the upright in the front room and began to play. Right away I could tell that he was so much better than most of the other casual players who'd been on the set. He played for a long time. I heard something different in the way he played, something new; a kind of modern touch I hadnt heard before, a certain feeling that I liked and wanted to learn. I thought feeling could be learned.

His name was Tull and he had at one time worked with some small bands out of New Orleans and Mobile, small combos mostly. He was really a trombone player but working out on piano was something of a hobby. "This is the way I relaxes myself," he told me.

Tull got into the habit of coming by just as the sun was going down to play ballads and blues for his own enjoyment for a couple of hours. Uncle Donald and Aunt Didi seemed to go for it too.

Uncle Donald would be moving thru the house, suspenders unhitched and shaving lather smeared all over his wide jaws, getting ready for another hard night. "Hey, do that one again, Tull," he'd call out from the bathroom if a number came up that he really liked. Tull would go into it again with that tough but gentle unheard-of touch of his.

I got into the habit of copping out of whatever game we kids happened to have going whenever he came over. There was a field next to the house where you could sit and still hear the music pouring from the livingroom window. I'd hide out there in the weeds and wig out.

Soon I overcame my shyness enough to ask Tull if I could watch him while he played. He was amused that a skinny brat like me should be interested in watching him play. I watched closely too, checking all his fingerings out, thinking he didnt know what I was up to. But he was on to me all along. "All right, son," he said one day, "tell you what. I'mo show you how this piece go and I'mo show it to you slow. Now, when I come back here tomorrow, I expect you to sit down and play it for me just like I taught it to you." He sucked at a can of beer and played me the chords and melody of a blues Ive never heard anywhere since. I sat down on the stool next to him and watched every move he made. "Think you got it now?"

"Nope, nossir, but I think I get the general idea."

"Lemme hear you play a little taste of it back

before I cut out cause I'm goin out on a run outta town and it aint no tellin when I might be back."

I made a couple of awkward attempts on the keys and stopped.

"Go on," Tull said, "that dont sound bad at all. Youll get it if you keep at it. Listen, just take your time, one note at a time over here with your right hand. Just take your time, that's all it is to playin the piano or anything else. Take your time and work it on out."

I went to bed that night feeling as if I had the key to all the secrets in the world.

"What you laughin to yourself about?" Jab asked me.

"Nothin."

"You are too. You got some money hid away, I betcha, that dont nobody know about."

"No, I'm just feelin pretty good, that's all."

"You cant jive me, you up to somethin, MC."

Inside of a week I had Tull's blues down pat and was making a nuisance of myself playing it over and over again around the house. I was waiting for him to turn back up so that he could listen to me. I knew he'd be proud.

Weeks went by and Tull didnt show. I went to Uncle Donald and asked about him. "O you mean Tull that use to come in here and be playin all that old good music on the piano? They got him over here in Louisiana or someplace, picked him up for somethin or other."

"Picked him up, sir?"

"That's right, picked him up."

"I dont think I know what you mean, Uncle Donald."

"I mean he in jail."

"In jail, what for?"

"Dont ask me."

"You mean they just put him in jail and dont nobody know what for? Did he rob somebody or kill somebody or somethin?"

Uncle Donald shook his head and yawned. "Learn to stay outta grown folkses business, boy. Scuse me, I have to go downtown and see a man about a dog."

FOUR

THE WAY Shakes walked and talked was music.

He was one of those freckle-faced Negroes with red hair. Shakes was short for Shakespeare whom he'd read as a child when he lived with his aunt, a part time Louisiana schoolmarm who kept a lot of books around the house. She made him sit by the woodstove after dinner and read, and she would reward him with spending change when he recited paragraphs and verses from the literature at hand—the Bible, Elizabethan plays and poetry, and writing by Abe Lincoln, Frederick Douglass, Booker T. and people like that.

By the time I'd settled back up north with Claude and met him, he wasnt reading much at all but still had a greedy memory and a razor tongue. I had been playing guitar for some time and had gotten to the point where I was thinking of getting an afterschool band together to play weekend jobs. I wanted Shakes to play drums but he didnt seem to be interested. Drumming in the school band was enough for him for the time being. He was involved with other things, namely girls, and didnt have time for much else. He loved talking about himself.

"Teacher told me I got a snapshot memory or somethin like that—you know, it work like a camera. I do things like memorizin the chart off the eye doctor's wall so I dont have to wear glasses, dig. I can remember stuff I read in a Captain Marvel or a Lone Ranger a long time ago when I wasnt nothin but a baby. I have a lotta fun, MC. Sometime I stop and try to figger out how I do it but that just make me cramp up in my mind and I cant remember nothin."

"Wow, well then you must get good grades behind all such as that!"

"Could if I wanted to but I dont. I cant stay innerested long enough."

"What is it you wanna do, man? You dont seem to like school, and you play some nice drums, if you ask me, but you dont seem to wanna do that either. What you wanna do?"

"I just wanna knock out chicks and show these other dudes they aint hittin on doodleysquat when it come to talkin trash. I got it down, jim! You hip to Cyrano de Bergerac? I musta seen that flick fifteen-twenty times. Talk about a joker could talk some trash! Cyrano got everybody told! Didnt nobody be messin with Cyrano, ugly as he was. Some silly stud get to cappin on Cyrano's nose and he dont flinch an inch. He get right up in the stud's face and vaporize him with several choice pronouncements, then he go and waste the cat in a suhword fight. Meantime, there's this little local lame that's tryna make it with Cyrano's cousin Roxanne, so old Cyrano and the lame get back up behind the bushes one night while the chick up there on the balcony. Cyrano whisperin all in the lame's ear what he spose to be sayin, but the lame messin up the lines so bad until Cyrano just sweep him on off to one side and stand up and make the speech his own self. He commence to messin up the broad's mind so bad she ready to out and out say *I do*. See, she dont know it's her own cousin that's been layin down that incredible rap. And now, to show you what kinda man Cyrano was, after the lady is on the verge of succumbing to the amorous design that his words had traced in the air of that night, so to speak, then he just step off to one side and let her old lame boyfriend move on into the picture and cop, like he the one been doin all that old freakish talk out there under the moonlight. Now, MC, you got to admit old Cyrano was a little taste outta the ordinary, now wasnt he? Tell the truth!"

"Yeah, I guess he was pretty way-out all right."

"Shhhoooot, he was more than just way-out. He was beautiful, that's what he was. Cyrano was one of them old exceptional cats it's lucky for us he got written up. That flick taught me a lesson. Taught me you can get away with anything if you talk up on it right. I got it down cold! I see me some square I dont too much go for and he up there with some sweet little thing, so I breaks over real casual-like, you understand, and put my sound in, right up under the square's nose." Shakes sighed. "Ahhh such is the simplicity of man to hearken after the flesh, if you can dig it. That I were more modest a lad than I appear to be. Thou art a bitch, Shakes, a stone bitch!"

We used to mess up a lot together. He was a good forger and would forge me perfect absence excuses for school. We'd skip school and do a lot of crazy things such as hang around in record shops catching all the new sounds, taking up the man's time. Or we'd go to movies, or plague the merchants of downtown Detroit, like the times we'd fall in J. L. Hudson's, the big department store, and steal silly things: pencil sharpeners, french-fry cutters, ties. I'd load up on paperbacks in the book section on the mezzanine, whispering things to Shakes like, "The Educated Fool strikes again."

There was a men's store just off Woodward Avenue with a vending machine that furnished free Vernor's ginger ale to its customers. We'd go up in there, buy thirty cents worth of handkerchiefs and drink a dollar's worth of ginger ale. That routine played out the afternoon we took Champ and some of his outrageous friends along equipped with canteens and thermos jugs. We cleaned the machine out in nothing flat and were promptly asked to leave and to never come back. The old saleslady was ready to sneak out back and ring up the police when she saw Shakes chug-a-lugging the last of the ginger ale from a papercup. He burped and looked straight at her. "I'm sorry, lady, I'm sincerely sorry but I dont think I could hold another drop."

Sometimes we'd just sit around calling up strange people from the telephone book. It didnt take us long to graduate from the gross prank-playing stage of having orders of ribs, chicken, shrimps and pizza dispatched to different parts of the city to the breaking up of marriages by faking the role of the wife's secret lover, mumbling grotesquely or hanging up when the husband answered. There was probably a phone company investigation underway to flush us out. But we only resorted to diversions of this kind when there was absolutely nothing else doing and we'd had a shot or so of Shakes' old man's whiskey or rum. This was also during the period that preceded our becoming involved with music to the point of feeling that little else mattered.

Strange, but it took a non-musician, a non-playing musician, at any rate, to wake us up to such things as jazz and the hip music show world. Even before getting to know Champ, however, we had already begun to play together more and more. We'd be beating around the streets on a weekday, a schoolday, phone Shakes' place and make sure his folks were away at work, break back up to his place and stand around listening to records or jiving one another. I started bringing my guitar with me. Gradually Shakes became interested in trying his hand at something besides the factory-arranged Sousa marches that the band at school was built around. We'd go down into his basement where the drums were set up and jam until the middle of the afternoon before getting nervous about his mother or father coming back home suddenly. This actually happened a couple of times.

One afternoon I had been feeling especially eager to play and had been out of school for several days recovering from a wisdom tooth extraction. Shakes happened to be absent at the same time on one of his famous one-week deals. He had told me, "It dont pay to be slippin out a day here and a day there because that way you end up spendin more time shuckin than it's worth. So I just come up with some kinda bigtime professional sickness and get that goin for me and then take a week or two out. See, that way I have time to get into a few things."

That afternoon had barely gotten underway. We were trying to perfect a catchy little piece that Shakes thought he'd written but which I recognized as being an ancient blues tune that my grandmother had at home in her and Bo's collection of old scratched-up 78s and 45s. It sounded something like *The Hucklebuck* except that it was trickier to play. It just so happened that we had been studying sodium and how, among other things, it was the base for sodium pentothal, truth serum, which was also a sedative. We were both just beginning to get interested in getting high and had brought home a small bag of sodium someone had swiped for us from chem lab at school. Shakes sprinkled a goodly amount into a frying pan with a few dashes of water and heated it over the stove until it began to steam. We leaned over the pan and inhaled the fumes violently until our nostrils stung, expecting to get a jag on of some kind. I got dizzy but that was about it. The frying pan had no sooner cooled and we had no sooner gotten back to playing when Shakes' mother, Mrs. Harris, came popping into the apartment home early from work. We heard her from the basement thunking around upstairs. She poked her head into the doorway leading down and hollered at us: "Hey! What's that funny smell that's all thru the house, and just what in the hell are yall doin home this time of day?"

"What you doin home, Mama?"

"Dont be askin me that, nigger, I'm *grown!* I come and go as I please. What I'd like to know is what *yall* doin up here home in the middle of the day? School let out early or somethin, or have you finally lost your mind? And dont be down there hollerin up at me, come on up here where I can see you!"

We bumbled up, Shakes talking to beat the band. "Well, Mama, MC here heard I was sick and he out from school cause he just had a tooth pulled and he thought he'd pay me a little visit and see how I was doin, isnt that right, man?"

"Yes, yes ma'am, that's right, Mrs. Harris."

Mrs. Harris slit her eyes and cut them my way

and, just like Claude's eyes, I could feel them penetrating me to the bone. It was useless, I knew, to try to put some shaky story over on her but I lied anyway. She nodded contemptuously at both of us and said, "I see. You just happened to stop by here with your guitar to pay James a visit, hunh?"

"Yes, ma'am."

"You niggers must think I'm blind, *must!* I can hear you clear down to the corner as I'm comin up the street and then get in here and the apartment smellin funny and yall think just cause you bout half-grown that I'm supposed to believe anything you tell me, is that it? Well, I aint going for it! *I am not going for it!* What *is* this mess anyway I smell floatin round thru here, what yall been up to?"

"Aw, Mama, that's just where me and MC fried us up some eggs and washed the pan out with a little Dutch cleanser and was lettin it heat on the stove so it would be easier to clean."

Shakes (James) could lie on moment's notice but Mama wasnt convinced. She could have called us on about fifteen counts of being wrong, but, perhaps because she was very tired, she said nothing except, "Well, I do not have the strength today to be arguin with you. I'll let your daddy fool with you when he get in—but I can tell you one thing: you gon have to pack your guitar up, MC, and cut your visit short. I have a headache and I cant stand no more racket right now, hear?" Then she sat down in a chair and told Shakes: "James, I'm just markin time till they graduate you from out of that school up there so I can call up the draft board and tell them to please come and get your lazy ass. Maybe the Army can do somethin with you, cause I dont think I can stand you much longer. Get on out of my sight—both of you!"

When we were off by ourselves, packing up, Shakes was sullen and concerned about the fuss that might be raised later when his father got home. "Sure wish she wouldnt bring my old man into this shit, MC. That dude is crazy. Last time we got into a thing we went down in the basement and he took off his belt and said he was gon whip my ass into bad health. I snatched the belt out his hand but he got a hammerlock on me and stood there talkin in my ear about, 'So you think you old enough to whip the old man, eh? You better check yourself and think about it some before you go tryna take me on man-to-man, son. Nigger, I'll whip the dudu outta you!' Tell you, MC, I been sizin the joker up and he still pretty big all right, always talkin bout how bad he was back when he was playin football—but you just wait. One of these days you gon pick up the paper and see a headline, *Son Beats Shit Out of Old Man,* and then you can just fold the paper up, you wont even have to read the story to know what's goin down. You just wait!"

FIVE

I WAS SHY but Shakes wasnt. When we were just getting out of junior high, he got hung up on a big girl in the eleventh grade. They had been making passes at one another for weeks and Shakes felt that it was time to get down to business but was nervous about it. "O would you believe it, MC lad, if your tender-bosomed sidekick Shakes were to intimate to you from the deeps of his lecherous old heart that all this despair that's been crampin his style is merely that he must needs purchase a container of much-needed prophylactics?"

He would actually come up with lines like that and bring them off the way he'd grin and wink at you afterwards, when all the words were out. It amazes me to this day that he didnt take up acting professionally.

We were downtown cutting thru old Grand Circus Park and it was February, freezing. "Why dont you go long with me, man. I never bought any of those things before."

I didnt know any more about it than he did but made an agreement. We began drifting from one drugstore to the next, putting it off.

"Look," I said finally, "next drugstore we go in youre gonna buy those damn trojans, and if youre too chicken to do it, I will. I cant stand all this foolin around."

"Thou dost speak masterly, lad. Come, let us seek out a merchant who will satisfy my fancy, for I must have them little things if I am to seal love's bonds new-made. Not I but my affairs have made you wait. Yon be a drugstore up there on the corner. Uh, prithee, let's make it."

"Want me to go with you?"

"Forget it, I think I done worked up enough nerve to handle this oneself. Just hang here outdoors, I'll be right out."

"All right, man, but it's cold out here!"

OK, that's me posted at the corner digging on all the frozen chickies rushing it home from work —and old Shakes has himself an eleventh-grader! I love them all as they shiver past prettied down with Ban, Lanvin, Arpège, Helena Rubinstein, Jergen's, Breck, Listerine, Colgate, Lysol, Hazel Bishop, Tintex, Playtex, seen with my mental Superman vision that cuts thru wool and fur, panty and bra—the sweet girl world when I was a boy.

Ten minutes in the cold and I had to rush inside to see what Shakes was up to. He hadnt bought anything. He was reading the colored magazines. "Man, why aint you bought the things, the raincoats?"

"You know, I was just about to do that little thing when this curious bit of journalism crossed my eyesight. Look here, I been readin this article about this dude that's a janitor for some big atomic radiation lavatory. Magazine musta thought it was cute cause he the only spook on the gig. Aint that a bitch! Think theyd print me up if I got on over at Buckingham Palace swabbin out toilets?"

"Aw, c'mon, man, let's take care of this business and get on back home."

"And look at this—a black French chef! Whatll they think of next? It's a lotta shades, you know, that still go for these old corny publications. You know who I mean—them saditty splibs, them e-lites that's so hung up on bein white that they cant even pronounce stuff right. They be talkin bout *marking bird* insteada mockin bird."

"Man, it's gettin late!"

"OK, OK, I'll do it on my own. Bear with me a minute till the druggist come out from behind there where he workin in the back gettin up them cures that work like a doctor's prescription."

We stand at the counter and wait. I rap on the glass with a dime. "Can I help you, boys?" It's a lady druggist.

Shakes says, "I, mmm, I dont know—how much are your, uh, coughdrops?"

"What he means, madam, is how much are your—that is . . . he'd like to buy some . . . ahhh—"

"Dont pay him no attention, lady, he doesnt know what I want."

That made me mad. I swallowed some phlegm and came right out with it—"A package of prophylactics please."

The lady turned red and smiled. "What size please?"

"What size? Woman, I dont know. Help me out, MC, what size you think I take?"

"Man, she means what size package you wanna buy!"

"O is that it? *Small,* I guess, smallest size you got, I dont care about the brand."

The nice lady tried to maintain her cool but we were too much for her. She cracked up right there on the spot, but came across with the goods. We handed over the money and got out.

Out on the streets, Shakes said, "MC, it gave me the creeps that woman lookin at me all suspicious like that."

"That was all in your head, man. What does she care? It was just another sale to her."

"Aw, that's just what you think, that's what's in *your* head. I bet she was wonderin if I'm old enough to be purchasin such contraceptive contraptions. You dont know these merchant class people like I do." He examined the flat little box. "I shoulda bought the giant economy size."

"What for? You got that much business to take care of?"

"Not hardly, but I feel like itd save me from havin to re-perpetrate this dastardly performance."

"True, but youll probably be grown by then anyway."

"I'm so hip!"

That's us, folks, making it to the nearest bus stop, laughing all over the sidewalk.

SIX

BUT LIFE was more than scenes and laughs, and, compared with Shakes, I suppose I was quite a gloomy customer.

Claude often told me that I took things too seriously. "You too serious, MC, for somebody your age. Me, I aint exactly ready for the cemetery yet, but I aint no child no more neither. Back when I was your age it wasnt too much they could come up with that would faze me."

It couldve been that, at sixteen, I thought I knew pretty much what it was all about. Besides playing the guitar, I was spending a lot of time in the public library peeking into books on my own. When I wasnt holed up at home by myself or with Shakes, practicing, or bopping around the neighborhood or downtown, the Detroit Public Library on Woodward Ave. was my home away from home. My thing was to go in there, dig up a book and sit in the music room reading while I listened thru earphones to a record. I didnt mind being with people but I liked being alone too.

Champ was a loner too, and, although he played no musical instrument, he became one of my main musical influences for a while by providing me with recordings I had never been consciously exposed to before. Teachers may not have thought so, but Champ was nobody's fool. He had his problems but, in many respects, was sharp and unique.

Until the semester we took swimming together, I had never really gotten a chance to know him. Occasionally he'd tip up behind me in the hall between classes, clamp his hands over my eyes and say, "Hey, guess who?" I'd sniff the odor of alcohol, tobacco, a hint of Juicy Fruit gum and answer, "Uhhh—Champ?" He got a big kick out of this and always acted surprised. "Say, howd you know it was me, man?"

He was a tall husky young man of ruddy, deep-brown complexion. He wore his hair in what I called a "semi-process" which is to say that he straightened his hair lightly, a little here, a little there, just enough to give the general effect of having fairly straight hair. It came out looking curly, coarse and weird.

I got into a fight with a white boy who'd been standing next to me at the lockerroom mirror one day. We were both combing our hair. "What's that stuff you use on your head," the white boy said, "Joe Louis Hair Pomade?"

I'm not quick-witted like Shakes and can rarely come up with the right thing to say at the right time, specially in a situation like that one, so, not being in the best of moods that morning, I carefully made a fist, keeping my thumb down as Jab had taught me long ago, drew back and bopped the boy in the mouth without saying anything—bam!—Farrell Katz, the biggest loudmouth in the class who was always trying to be a comedian, Jerry Lewis or somebody; the only person Ive ever hit in my life. If I had thought for a moment, I never would have done it.

Farrell wiped blood from his lip with the back of one hand and said in a trembly voice, "I was just kidding, man, I was just kidding, you know, cant you take a joke for chrissake!"

"I'm sorry, Farrell," I told him in just as shaky a voice, "but you shouldntve said that. That was just the wrong thing to say."

It would have been nothing more than another incident had it not been for the fact that both Dick the black lockeroom attendant and Champ had been looking on.

Dick was cool. I have always been thankful for his coolness in not making a big thing out of the incident because he just as easily could have turned me in to the swimming coach Mr. Dangle who would have taken me up to Mr. Brown the principal. I could have been expelled. As it turned out, Dick walked over calmly, spent a long time checking out Farrell Katz's busted lip, hauled us both off into a little side room where he applied first aid to Farrell's cut and heartily reprimanded me in front of him. "I want you to apologize to this boy, MC."

I told him I had already apologized.

"Then do it again so I can hear you. That was a terrible thing you did just now."

"Well, I'm sorry, man," I told Farrell again, "but you were wrong, you were wrong and I just couldnt take what you said to me."

Farrell's jaws were tight. He got a little wet in

the eyes and told me it was OK, that he hadnt meant anything by the remark and that he wouldnt hold it against me. But he never even spoke to me again the whole time we were in school.

Many of us were given to making remarks and joking about one another's hair down in the lockerroom, as we were coming out of the showers, say. Fights would break out. Dick, the attendant, was a lightskinned balding man in his middle forties who finally got a bunch of us off in a corner and told us, "Listen, I want you kids to stop talking about one another's grades of hair because the first thing you know one of these little white boys is gonna pick it up and say something and then youre gonna wanna bust him one. So quit doing it, it's ugly and it's unnecessary. Cant none of us help having the kind of hair we've got, we were born with it. There isnt any such thing as good or bad hair!"

One of the fellows made some crack about Dick not having very much hair of any kind left. Dick turned crimson in the face and challenged whoever it was to a physical contest right then and there. "You wanna step outside and throw hands with me, son? Right now? Do you?"

"Nossir . . ."

"Then check your mouth! I'm trying to talk to you like you got some sense, and if you take my advice youll cut out some of this capping on one another and playing the dozens and be proud of what you are! We've got a lot to be proud of, you know. We're Afro-Americans, black people, and it's time we started taking a little pride in ourselves, do you hear me? You might understand what Ive been trying to tell you one of these days —if youre lucky! But now, look here—if somebody wants to get smart with me, I'm ready for that too. I might look like a fool but push come to shove I'll duke a few rounds with anybody here. And I dont play! I'll crack some head in a minute! I'll smack the chicken hockey outta you, come getting smart with me! Hell, I'm a grown man, I dont be playing with no kids!"

Champ was grown too as far as we were concerned, and he was someone else you didnt play with. Super cool, the only thing he ever said to me about the Joe Louis Hair Pomade incident was: "Mmmm, MC, I was checkin it out—nice, niiiice! I think you probly saved the cat from a awful beatin splittin him in his jibs right quick like that. Yeahhh—"

Except for the semester he was forced to take swimming, Champ would always suit up in the lockerroom and go upstairs to the gym to find himself an inconspicuous spot where he could hide out, usually ending up upstairs in the shadows of the track above the gym floor. While the rest of us knocked ourselves out playing basketball, dodgeball, whatever the instructor had on his agenda, Champ would sleep away the hour.

When the weather was warm and gym class was moved outdoors for baseball, soccer or touch football on the playground, Champ would find himself a nice spot away from all the tussle where he could nap in the shade or smoke, sit, and daydream at the ground. He was always tired because he stayed out late at night hanging out with grown men in cafés, bars, dance halls, poolrooms. He drank a lot of sweet wine.

"Fellas," he'd proclaim, plopped on the locker-room bench, lacing up a shoe, "it aint nothin like that pluck to snatch you in place." Pluck was wine, usually Bird, Thunderbird. "Unless you know someplace where we can score for some gangster—and then you talk about gettin straight for real, oooooweeee! That good gauge'll straighten anybody out in a minute!" He'd laugh off to one side in that noddy way of his and say something like, "Yeahhh, straighten you out and jeck you around too."

Champ had flunked grades left and right but had made it on into high school, and there he was with the rest of us, another generation. "School dont bother me none. I aint in no hurry to get outta this rathole. I know what's happenin. Shee-it, this the best time of my life and you better believe I know it too. Every time they call theyself gon ease me on outta here, I eases right back in some kinda way. Now they just leave me alone which is all I ever wanted em to do in the first place. My old lady all the time tryna get me to join the service, but I done been thru that change too and they dont want me neither, say I got a bad attitude."

SEVEN

CHAMP TURNED both me and Shakes on to some of the beautiful sounds that were floating around that we had never truly gotten into.

Some of that music, jazz mostly, really turned me around the first time I stopped and started listening to it. There are tunes that still conjure up the way I was feeling, the change that was coming over me in those lonely, silly days. When I hear some of that music, I can even remember the way rain fell, little patches of muddy snow melting under streetlights, the smell of gasoline in spring; vibraphone solos being blown from loudspeakers hung outside record shops; the way chicks came out of those enormous coats in April, thinned down, and started looking good again; Claude grumbling at the TV way into the night while 45s and LPs spun out of my room—"MC, you losin your mind! I aint got but bout one nerve left and you gettin on *that!* Turn that damn victrola down!"

This is some of what comes to mind when I think of those wild, impressive, heartbreaking days when I first began to thrive on sounds. Ideas, feelings, everything was connected to sounds, to song, a chord cluster, rapid-fire solo breaks, slow sneaky melody lines, counterpoint (which I read all about in the library listening to so-called serious music).

Have you ever been young and sat in your room in a city with the lights out around the time it's beginning to get dark outside and checked out the world trickling past your window to the rush and flow of powerful sounds? I have. I got into that. I got way off into that.

I first got to talk to Champ in swimming class. We had both been benched—me for just a week with a light cold, Champ because he'd come close to drowning one session and had blamed the instructor, Mr. Dangle, who, I must confess, was given to some pretty sloppy supervision. Champ definitely might have drowned that morning had it not been for some fast thinking and action on the part of Phil Wyzinski who dived in and pulled Champ out of the water before Mr. Dangle could even bring himself to fold away his *Detroit Free Press* and scare up a life preserver. Champ's last public words to Mr. Dangle had been: "Just as soon as I get myself together and get some of this chlorine and shit pumped outta my lungs—and can stand on my own two feet without havin to lean on nobody—I am def-fin-nit-lee go-ing to kick you dead in your ass!"

But the case had been taken up to Mr. Brown, the principal, who was no ordinary hot-headed functionary but a man who could see that things could go bad for him and the school if it got out that a student had come close to drowning in class because of the negligence of a swimming instructor. And a disadvantaged black student at that, even if he *was* crazy! Mr. Brown must have handled matters smoothly because Dangle ended up apologizing to Champ as well as to Champ's only parent, his mother, and never again did he doze over newspapers or magazines during class. Brown later proved his slickness by running for congressman in our basically non-white district, and winning.

Champ came to class but didnt have to do anything. He sniffed and turned the pages of a magazine.

"What's that you readin, Champ?"

"Lookin at this *Down Beat.*"

"Is it good?"

"I dont know. I just like to pick up on what everybody be doin, y'understand. They got in here where all the scenes is and who the people are that be on the scene and what they got to say about it, all such illy-gump as that."

Champ spoke that bad central city argot, that tight, clipped, acid, hard hip lingo that's calculated to keep outsiders in their place minding their own business.

"What scene?"

"What scene? Man, you mean you dont know?"

"I know what scene means but I dont know what youre talkin about."

"Well now." He slid into that sleepy, whispery chuckle of his, a cross between Ha-Ha-Ha and Kiss-My-Ass. "You dig on much modern jazz?"

"I kinda go for jazz, unh-hunh, but I like blues too, rhythm and blues, you know."

"Yeah, I know—that shit they be blastin over Poppin Percy's Show. I can go for some of that too when it's a group that's got somethin goin for em beside a lotta doo-wah. But I'm talkin about jazz, baby, modern jazz, some call it contemporary. It aint but one jazz far as I'm concerned. I aint talkin bout all this old rickytick that ofays play and rebop and bebop and shit. I'm talkin bout what's happenin now, right this now, *modern,* can you dig it?"

"Yes, I think I know what you mean."

"Lemme break it down for you some more. Now, you take me—I go for sounds. People all the time be wonderin how come I'm all the time hunched over got my eyes closed or look like I be thinkin real deep bout somethin—well, I be's thinkin bout them sounds, MC. I be's thinkin bout all the tough and fantastic sounds that these old lame jive-ass motherfuckers aint never heard *tell* of much less *heard.* You know, I be's groovin behind what's swishin round up in my dome, dig it?"

"Yeah, I can dig it," I told him hurriedly, trying to think up a new subject we could get on. Champ was getting worked up and had a scary look in his eyes that made me uncomfortable because I didnt know just how to take it. As he flipped thru the *Down Beat,* I got a glimpse of someone playing guitar. "Is there much about guitar playin in there? That's what I play."

Quite suddenly, and for no reason I could think of, he handed me the mag and then rubbed his face in his hands and yawned. "Here, you can have it—it's yours, man. I got two of em anyway."

"What you doin with two of em?"

"I copped one up at Thad's drugstore the other night and then went and forgot and up and copped another one someplace else. I was loaded back, man, I thought it was a different one. I like to look thru them books every once in a while but you dont need to read that jive they got in here just to pick up on what's going down tho. Other night I got me some white port and some lemon juice and smoked me some boo—that's what keep me goin, brew, boo and bobbycue—and then I dropped some sounds on the box and maaaaan, I didnt know where the hell I was. I mean I was out there, jim, I was bout a lost motherfucker! Tell you, I was so messed up until even after the recordplayer'd done turnt itself off I was still turned on, got all them sounds going round up in my head like that, like I was inside a echo chamber or off top of some mountain someplace, man, I was fuhhhhhked-up!"

I had to close the mag and listen. He told me about his life at home. "You dont catch me hangin round the crib that much—it aint too much to do round there. My old lady, she OK, you know, but she kinda stiff, you know—she dont know what's goin on—I mean, she all the time talkin bout what's done happened and I'm steady lookin after what's happenin, y'understand. She dont understand nothin I do and she bug me somethin terrible, man, all the time pullin on my coat tryna get me to do this and to do that—Go get a job and get thru school, you aint got good sense, you just like your old good-for-nothing old man!—and all that kinda sound, you hip to it? Who wanna all the time be listenin to that? So you know what I did?" For the first time since I'd known him, Champ gave me an out and out smile. "Know what I did, man? I got back there up in my room, dig, and I got me some thick black tape, you know that old black sticky tape—and I got me some black kinda plastic stuff and I stuck that jive up all over my windows, all round the edges of the door and everyplace I could think of so couldnt no light get in, and then I put another lock on my door and put in some blue lightbulbs—you followin me?—and then I got back up in there, man, when I'm back up in there now, I mean, it's just me and my scene. It's my thing, jim! I be's out to lunch! I'll play me some LPs and shit and maybe smoke me some charge or knock off a little pluck or drop a coupla goofballs or whatever the fuck I feel like doin, and dont *nobody* be fuckin with me. Get them sounds goin and sometime I be back up in there all night it get so good to me, MC—all them freakish sounds and all that groovy feelin be buzzin thru me. It brings a good feelin, I can tell you that, it do bring a good feelin, warm kinda feelin."

I thought of my own dream of having a soundproofed room where I could practice my guitar all night if I wanted and not have Claude on my back about noise.

"Now, that's just when I'm home I be into that, but, like I say, I dont be home all that much. I like to run over here to the Greystone sometime and check out the haps when somebody that's any good hit town and play there, or either maybe get together and hit the streets with Andy Coleman or Wimp when they aint giggin someplace, or Captain Midnight, Mister McGoo or Cha-Cha—altho Cha-Cha been going thru some old *other* kinda changes lately—them sóme crazy niggers, damn! Talk about crazy, them some off-the-wall scogues all right. They dont even be making sense to one another much less to other boots and some of these simple-ass grays. Get holda me a coupla dollars and I might cut over on John R. or back over here to 12th Street and talk some old nickel ho into runnin round with me to catch a few sets but, maaaaan, some of them silly bitches can get me drugger than a motherfucker. All most of em know to do is spend bread, want you to all the time be droppin that coin on em and even then it's a lot of em still dont wanna get up off no trim, shee-it, tighten my jaws!"

"Do you play anything yourself?" I asked, sensing that he was probably in as good a mood as he'd ever be.

"Naw, baby, I dont play nothin but I ought to. My old lady messed me up, you know. When I was back in the fifth grade—and take it from me, when I was in the fifth grade that was a long time ago. Teacher brought a bunch of us up to this band room and had us tryin out some of the instruments. The dude was even studyin me while I was testin out tubas and trumpets and basses and drums and trombones and everything and told me I oughta be blowin clarinet or sax, said I had a feel for reeds, y'understand, said it might even help keep me innerested in school. But my old lady, that chick, man, she thought he didnt know what he was talking bout, said we couldnt afford no instrument even if it had to come from out the pawnshop. So now here I am, all fucked up, cant play nothing but the radio, the recordplayer and the TV. You taught yourself to play the guitar, hunh?"

"No, one of my grandmama's people started me off on it."

"Where was he from—downsouth someplace?"

"Mississippi."

"I knew it, I knew it! Them old dudes can play, cant they? I got a uncle come from down outta there someplace—Georgia—joker can reach over and grab hold of a trombone and blow the shit out of it. Grab anything, shooooot, grab a jug, a coffee cup, rubberband, anything—grab one of them life preservers out there in the pool there and blow it to pieces. He dont be jivin neither, the cat's a musician, a natural musician. He pick up one of these plastic ukuleles from out the dimestore and play some old funkybutt blues make you cry."

"Say, Champ, I sure would like to hear some of your records sometime. I really havent heard too much of this really modern stuff."

"Aint too many people really heard it, baby. They might listen to it but they dont be hearin it. I'd tell you to come by the pad, I live right down the street from Shakes there, but my old lady got her mouth stuck out half the time and she always scared somebody gon try to break in. She kinda weird, y'understand, and since I dont be there all that much she dont dig on people just up and fallin by. So, why dont I bring a coupla LPs to school one day and you can take em on home and check em out—if you got a good needle, dont be layin no bogue needles on my choice jams, man! I got a gang of em too."

"Hey, nice, man—but cant I bring you something for exchange, like? All we have are mostly old blues and pop and those old jump records that belong to my folks, a lotta rhythm and blues and that kinda thing."

"I know—all them old rock jams and shit, all that ram-de-bam and oompty-doomp, unh-unh, baby, I been thru that. I'll just loan you some of my albums. You might even be able to cop some ideas or tunes to play off of em. How that sound?"

I was moved by his unexpected kindness and interest in my playing. "OK, Champ, but if there's anything I can do, any favors or anything like that, just let me know."

He looked thoughtfully toward Phil Wyzinski, his one-time savior, who was taking a running dive off the board. "Now, you see that boy there? That's a OK dude for a gray cat." His attention shifted back to me. "Look here, you say you wanna pay me back for some of them jams I'mo bring you to hear?"

"Sure, what you got in mind?"

"Why dont you start by lettin me have this fifteen cents so I can buy me some milk or pie or somethin for lunch. All I had for breakfast was a

Pepsi and a coupla spoons of chili my old lady had left over in the icebox. My damn stomach sound like it's fixin to erupt!"

"Here you go," I said, handing over the last of my paper route money for the week. "Will fifty cents do?"

"That all you got?"

"Yeah, but–"

"How bout you let me have a quarter and you keep a quarter. How the hell you gon eat if you gimme all your bread, shee-it."

EIGHT

So, UP until Champ, I had never thought about music as a way of life. He seemed to have gotten the way he dressed, the way he moved, the tone of voice in which he spoke, so much of his style seemed to have come from the music he liked. I realized this more and more as I listened to the records he loaned me, many of them remarkable sounds that went beautifully thru me. I also realized the countless possibilities of music as a way of life, there being as many ways of life as there were people, as there were lives. The question became: What was going to be my own way of life?

What were other people doing? How did they see themselves?

One morning I was reading *The Question Man* in the paper. The question for the day was: "Do You Think of Yourself as Average?"

I didnt know if I was average or not. The question had no meaning for me. I'd tried but just couldnt seem to pass myself off as average. No one that I knew, for that matter, seemed average to me: Claude, Shakes, Champ. No one.

Claude didnt like the average, corny music that most people went for, but she wasnt crazy about the stuff I was bringing home lately either. "Where you gettin all that outrageous mess from anyway? You gon lose your mind, MC, you keep on listenin to that noise! It aint nothin but a lotta racket and I wish you would quit torturin *me* with it! Lord knows I got enough to worry with without that. That's worse than that old bebop and junk they was playin back when I was comin along."

Average or not—up until Champ, I was pretty lame, all things considered, a real dude.

I minded my grandmother, I read a lot, I listened to music and worshipped rhythm and blues musicians (one of the reasons I got interested in guitar), and I never gave much thought to what I would do once I got out of school. I thought vaguely of joining a band and going away, but it was more of a daydream than anything else. In this daydream, some noted musician, from New York, say, was forever urging me to wind up my affairs in this big country town and sign with him to play the top spots in the country. But in my heart I couldnt help wondering what would become of Claude left all by herself.

We didnt have that much. We didnt have a car or modern furniture or fancy clothes. Everything we had was plain: black and white TV, monaural, bathtub instead of a shower, steam heat. Claude wasnt that big on owning things; her numbers dream was to hit for enough to not have to work so hard so that she would have time for other things. Eventually she wanted to go back to school and finish up her high school education. She also spoke of becoming a seamstress and earning a living that way and not have to get up and go punch anybody's damn timeclock, but such dreams, to come true, needed money behind them. At least she wasnt like Aunt Didi who, once she and Uncle Donald made a little money, started buying new furniture and covering it with plastic. You could never really relax in their house for fear that you'd mess everything up, or that the couch would get greasy and crash to the floor the minute you got comfortable on it.

"It's people in this world aint even got as much as we got," Claude always reminded me. Just the same, I believed that one of the things that kept me from being one of the boys was the fact that my clothes looked funny. A lot of them were old and had been retailored by Claude. She wasnt a bad seamstress, but I wanted to get in on some of the clothes other kids were wearing, ridiculous fashions from Hot Sam's downtown or from some of the tacky shops on 12th that catered to and even helped form much of the Sunday illustrated taste of kids in my neck of the woods.

On the other hand, I never looked truly unkempt or poor; just peculiar, a little offbeat. I didnt go around raggedy like poor Logan Jones, who played baritone horn in the band at school, and his brothers. The kids in Logan's family wore gym shoes all the time, in gym class and out, summer and winter. "Seymour shoes!" somebody cracked cruelly. "Seymour foot than you do shoe."

What we did have Claude kept clean, dusted and in good repair. We saved money not having a car. After what had happened to Pancho and Flo, she never wanted to drive again. Bo had driven when he was alive, but now Claude was content to take the bus everywhere.

Me, I was a nice kid who played music instead of the dozens—and with records and books instead of with girls.

Donna Lee Jackson, who lived on the east side but went to our school on the west side, had a thing for me, according to Shakes, but I was too goofy to go to the trouble of trying to get next to her. And I dug Donna Lee almost as much as I did my guitar.

PART TWO

ONE

CHAMP WAS neither here nor there but everywhere. Since he ran, for the most part, with an older crowd, he really didnt have much time for kids, for people like Shakes and myself, but often we'd get together to listen to music, or sometimes Champ would come by to hear us practice. We thought we were getting to be pretty good.

"How you think we sound, man?" I asked him after a particularly grueling workout we'd put ourselves thru one evening down in Shakes' basement.

Champ had been sitting quietly in one corner letting his head wobble discreetly and nipping at some Manischewitz wine Shakes had sneaked for him from upstairs. "You wanna know what I think?" he said, rubbing his jaw thoughtfully with one hand and staring down into the palm afterward as though an answer had been written there. "Fellas, it's like this. Now, dont get me wrong. I dont want you to go jumpin all jiggedy just cause I tell you this."

Shakes was indignant. "Aw, this nigger talk like he fixin to come up with some kinda critique or somethin."

"Wait a minute, Mr. Shakespeare, I aint said nothin yet!"

"Be quiet, Shakes, and let the cat say what he's got to say."

Champ really worked it up into a production. He rose from his seat and paced the floor, rubbing his hands together, pausing for a moment near the drums or near me where I was sitting with my guitar across my knee. He seemed to be mulling over the shape of each instrument.

Shakes said, "I dont know about you, MC, but I got some homework to do. I'm goin back upstairs. You can stay here while this joker go thru his act."

"Dig up," Champ said finally. "Tell you, here's how I feel about you guys' music–since you asked. I think you dudes got a pretty good little thing goin, really. I mean, you got possibilities. But see, since yall been tryna get into all this modern shit I been slippin down to you, I think you oughta spend more time round modern musicians. Yall should pick up on more live music–man, I dont care how good somethin be soundin on a record it's always badder when you catch it in person. Even a dude that dont play all that good he sound better live sometime than somebody great that's just on a record. Yall got your instruments down under control but now you got to learn to get on down inside yourself. That's where it's at, if you can dig it. Course, I aint no musician.

I lit up inside. "I can dig what you tryna say."

"I dont mean to come on salty or nothin," said Shakes, "but, like, if you supposed to be all that bad and deep then how come you dont play nothing yourself?"

"Everybody doesnt have to play just to tell you what they like," I shot back in Champ's defense, feeling that Shakes had no right to be so pushed-out and arrogant.

Champ just gave that airy laugh of his from way down in his throat but there wasnt much of the Ha-Ha-Ha in it. "Listen," he said, smacking his lips on a fresh sip of Concord grape wine, "I know some cats I think yall should come around and meet and get to know. They musicians too but they older dudes and they together, man. They be workin gigs and everything."

Shakes was still upset "How come we gotta go over and be diggin on somebody else? What's the matter with our shit?"

"Aint nothin wrong with the way yall play—it's just I think you could stand gettin exposed to a little live action, that's all. Have you ever been to any clubs or concerts or anything like that?"

"You know we arent old enough to be gettin in clubs and places," I said.

"That's what I mean. I might can get yall into some places or introduce you to some of the people that's on the set that can maybe pull your coats to some good things, Mr. Shakespeare."

"All right, OK," Shakes said, "but on the other hand"—(he let a drumstick fall from one hand into the other and the tension between him and Champ lightened)—"on the other hand, I d(see what make you think you can come up in here in *my* house and drink *my* wine and breathe your old nasty breath all up in *my* face and tell me that *my* playin aint together—or, shall we say, leaves something to be desired."

"You mean come here in your old man's house and drink your old man's wine," I said, but I knew what Shakes was going to say next, so I began to unplug and pack up.

"Man, I guess I must not be gettin to you," Champ broke out, somewhat apologetic. "I wasnt puttin your drummin down. I was just—"

"Nope, sorry, I wont hear any of it, ace. Methinks indeed that one day perhaps I shall be able to dig upon thee. But thou for now hast messeth with my tender feelings, blackamoor, and I'm wont to question thy damn motives. Has it not been explained to thee how remarkably close I have come to being one of the world's great drummers?"

"Say, whuhhhhh . . . ?"

"I wouldnt pay him too much mind," I told Champ, arranging my guitar in its old beatup hard case.

"Aint no big thing," Champ said, winking at me in mock contempt. "It's just like I always thought." He shielded his mouth with the back of his hand and spoke over his shoulder to me. "This little red nigger think he cute."

TWO

THE NIGGER who thought he was cute and I started seeing quite a bit of Champ and hanging with him whenever he'd let us. He'd fall by my place once or twice a week and terrorize Claude, get her all worked up. She wasnt particularly impressed by Champ with his long leather coat, knob-toed Stacy Adams, stingy-brim pulled down over his head. He had a bad habit of popping by at the oddest hours, jaws crammed back with chewing gum and a toothpick munched all the way up to the tip which poked prominently out from one side of his mouth. His slum majesty! "Uhh, excuse me, Moms, but is MC home?"

At first Claude wouldn't show him in. If I happened to be around the house, she'd make him wait at the door, outside on the porch, while she went to get me. Her face would be very stiff. "It's somebody at the door wanna see you." Later, however, as she became resigned to his coming around, she'd simply open the door, not say a word, and point back toward my room. In a good mood she might add, "I reckon he back up in there someplace."

It took some time for her to attain this disposition of relative calm. First of all, I had to break

Champ up from calling her *Moms*. Claude resented that violently and told me so when we were alone. "For the last time, MC, if you got to have that old pimpish-lookin nigger comin round here, would you please set him straight about what my name is. My name is not Moms, and if he keep on callin me that he gon show up at the door one of these days and I'mo haul off and dash a whole bucket of hot lye smack in his face. I hate to have to say somethin like that cause I know it's not the Christian thing to be thinkin but I dont like nobody that take me to play with. He gets me sick! My name is Claudette Moore and it's all right for you to call me Claude but I think he oughtta have enough respect to know to call me Mrs. Moore. I cant stand the Negro, and I wish you would stop hangin round with him. What is it about him that fascinate you so much in the first place?"

"Aw, Claude, he's pretty up on music and stuff, that's all. He's got a lotta records and I'm learnin a lot from the music he lends me."

"Well, if that's all he got to offer, then why dont you and Shakes get a job in a record shop? Yall can go right up here to Rodney's Records and get a part-time job after school and hear all the ram-de-bam and nut music yall's poor hearts can take."

"That isnt the point."

"Then what *is* the point if you dont mind my askin—for you to be layin out all hours, at *all* hours of the night with, with Chimp?"

"Claude, his name is Champ."

"I know what he call hisself—but to me he favor a chimpanzee in the face."

Claude stayed on that kick the whole summer Shakes and I were seeing a lot of Champ. The mention of his name was enough to throw her into a lightweight bind.

In he comes, doing that rhythmic walk, *macking* they called it; one arm stiff at his side, the fingers curled up, a paperbag or box of some kind in his other arm, jaws working steadily on that gum. If he isnt wearing leather he's got on his trench-coat. He macks into my room where the sounds are, takes a seat on the edge of the bed, empties his pockets, spreads it all out: packs of different brands of cigarettes, candies, gums, plastic center inserts for 45 rpm records, cigarette paper, matches, ticket stubs, scraps of paper with names and addresses on them, an orange, maybe a pint whiskey bottle that's been refilled with sherry or muscatel—I cant tell you what-all. He takes a sip and offers me some which I accept sometimes, popping a chlorophyll gumdrop into my mouth, figuring it's better to go around green-tongued than to have Claude down my throat about reek-ing of drink—and down we settle for a hard few hours of digging sounds. Often I play along on guitar with records, the simpler, easy to follow ones, while Champ lingers around the room en-tranced, or lies back across the bed, moving only his head or feet or tapping his fingertips together in time to the music. Occasionally he rises to make some point, or to emphasize some specific part of a chorus, or to register enthusiasm for something I'd done. "Hey, what was that little thing you did just now—yeahhh, niiiiice, baby, niiiiice! You startin to stretch out now. Go put that cut back on, that Wes Montgomery and dig where he be doin that old funnytime break on that thing, forget what you call it, *mmmm*." That little *mmmm* was something that got tagged on to everything he said when he was high.

Lots of times Shakes would be up in there with us. He wouldnt have his drums but would sit in a corner and work out on the bottom of one of my wooden chairs or a box, any old thing. I'd be picking and chording and Champ, poor Champ who wanted to play an instrument so badly, would stand around working his arms and fingers for hours sometimes, shaping the smoky air in the room into some imaginary saxophone, trumpet, flute, trombone, piano, bass, anything but drums or guitar which he figured we had covered. Dramatically he'd go thru the motions of mimicking the sounds that rolled off the records.

We all wanted to get good, split town, cut records ourselves and just stand around clean and hip, basking in limelight.

THREE

CHAMP WOULD disappear for days at a time and then turn up with no explanation as to where he'd been, what he'd been doing.

Once he vanished for two full weeks before Shakes and I ran into him on 12th Street talking with a white man in front of the Cream of Michigan Café. We spotted him from across the street. It looked as if he and the man were finishing up a transaction of some kind. We jaywalked over to say hello. The white man cut out. "Champ! Hey, Champ!"

"Say, my main men," he drawled, flashing an uneven grin at each of us and giving us what Shakes called the chump-squeeze, a momentary five-fingered pinch on the arm or shoulder that meant whatever you wanted it to mean. Shakes always put it on bow-tied hawkers of *Muhammad Speaks* when they confronted him at corners and he was short of money—that brisk squeeze coupled with a polite "I already checked that issue out, Brother, and it's beautiful, I'm in there wi'cha all the way!" usually did the trick.

"If it aint my good musician partners, MC and Shakes! What yall doin round here this time of night?"

"Just walkin around standin out in front of the joints checkin out the sounds."

"Know what you mean. I do the same thing myself when it aint nothin better to do. How yall doin with your drums and shit?"

"We been writin a lotta tunes, man, a lotta blues mostly but it's comin along."

It was a cool night in late summer and Champ was togged down in his lightweight trench, his stingy-brim and coal-black shades.

"You subject to get arrested, Champ," I told him, "goin round here at night with shades on that dark. The man is subject to put you way back up in the jail."

"Yeah, well, that wouldnt be so bad with me just so long as I could keep on feelin good as I do. Look here!" He motioned us closer and dropped his voice to a coarse whisper. "Do yall turn on?"

Shakes looked at me and I at him. Shakes said, "Turn on with what?"

"Shh, shh, dont be talkin so loud or we'll be arrested sure enough! Look, I got holda some gangster that wont stop. A coupla tokes of this shit and that's all she rote! Talk about spendin a night in Tunisia, this some shit come straight outta Hong Kong by way of California or someplace and they tell me it's been cured in opium. I aint never smoked nothin come on this strong!"

Shakes was all for it but I had reservations. It was already pushing ten and I usually tried to get home no later than eleven-thirty because I got up mornings before dawn to take care of my paper route.

Champ took note of my hesitancy and said, "It's all right, MC, this aint no skag or nothin, just a little pot to open your head up some, let you dig a little more—and yall call yallselves musicians, I know you wanna get your ears opened up so you can hear some of this jive the way it's supposed to be heard. I wouldnt put you in no kinda trick, honest, *plus* I aint gon even charge you a dime. I just wanna see you dudes lit up for a change, my treat!"

I kept on hemming and hawing but Shakes said, "MC, long as I been knowin you, you aint never done nothin that smacked of adventure. Damn, let's adventure a little taste and see what it's like. Ive done it before. It's better than gettin drunk. See you think it's like gettin drunk and it aint."

"Naw, it aint," Champ added, shifting his eyes this way and that. "Fact, I know some broads live round the corner on Euclid where we can go do up a coupla joints. It wont take but bout ten-fifteen minutes. C'mon."

He started walking and we fell in behind and beside him, no one saying much of anything anymore, and me growing fluttery inside, imagining what it was going to be like, and worried about getting home OK. We moved past the shrimp shacks, rib joints, record shops, bars and crowds of people in the street, made a turn on Euclid and walked until we came to a big apartment building. Champ pressed out a code on the buzzer and soon the door buzzed back.

FOUR

THE PERFUMED GIRL who answered upstairs was cute, short-haired and mahogany-colored with perfect teeth. She reminded me of Donna Lee except Donna was prettier. She and Champ were obviously old friends. He grinned, pushed back his stingy-brim and said, "Claire Howard, you old foxy ho! OK if we fall on in and do up a coupla numbers if we stay in the kitchen and dont interfere with what yall got goin on?"

"What you got?" Claire asked Champ, talking past him actually while she checked me and Shakes out.

"Just a coupla joints, but you talk about some baaaaad reefer!"

There were two other girls fidgeting around in another room, the livingroom. Claire asked us in and introduced us. One girl, a pert little black gal in a bright store wig, was named Michele. The other was named Leona and she was lightskinned, shapely but hefty, and she chewed and snapped her gum more mercilessly than Champ.

Claire said, "Champ, we expectin some company soon and you know Geechy dont like to have strangers comin up here if it's not on business."

"Now, baby, who the one that always turns you

on when you down to your last matchbox? Who the one that got your purse back the time it got snatched down here on Clairmount? Who the one that lays all them new jams on you that he cops out the shops and dont ask nothin in return, never?"

Michele and Leona didnt pay much attention to us. Skinny Michele, in her short mumu and fishnet stockings, was reading *TV Guide* and smoking. Leona, in black slacks and a cashmere sweater, had her shoes off and was painting her toenails silver. "What Champ want, Claire?"

"He brought these boys up here and they all wanna turn on out in the kitchen."

Michele seemed disturbed. "Theyre just kids, Champ, it look like to me. Man, we got enough trouble without you bringin us some more. If they wanna do some business, that's one thing. We fixin to get ready to go out. If Geechy come up here and catch yall smokin and carryin on he gon raise natural hell and we the ones end up gettin our ass kicked."

Champ motioned for me and Shakes to stay back near the door and got all the chicks around him in a circle. He addressed himself almost exclusively to Claire who seemed to head the pack. "Listen, lovelies, these dudes is friendsa mine and I'll vouch for em. That one there is MC, he play guitar, and the little red nigger name Shakes and he can play some drums and a half when he feel like it. Now Geechy know me and I know Geechy. Fact, I'm the one introduced *you* to Geechy, Miss Michele, so you aint got no business comin on to me with that bad attitude of yours. Now, can we come in and behave like gentlemen or am I gon have to pitch one and get all yall cussed out? When I come up here I thought maybe yall might not mind hittin a toke or two yourself of this weed, but now you gettin me mad, shee-it."

The girls all looked at one another. Claire blinked her eyes at me extra hard as though she were trying to come to some decision. Finally she said, "I dont mind you turnin on up here, Champ, and this one that you say play drums he look all right, but this other one here look like he aint never smoked no pot or done nothin like that in his life."

Leona, headed back toward the rear of the apartment, said, "Aw, Claire, Champ say they musicians so they must be into *some*thin. I say let em on in and if Geechy come in with his mouth stuck out, let Champ do the explainin. I dont know bout yall but I'm gettin out here in this street and see if I cant get some action together. All I ask, Champ, is will yall please take care your little business and get the hell outta here cause it freaks customers out when I bring em up here and it's somethin funny goin on."

Both Leona and Michele cut out.

Claire wouldnt stop looking at me, but she no longer seemed hostile or suspicious. "This one," she said, nodding toward me, "is kinda cute. What you say his name was?"

"MC, this is Claire. Claire, MC."

"How you doin, MC?"

"I'm all right. How you doin?"

"What do the MC stand for?"

"Stands for MC, that's all, just MC."

"One of them oldtime names, hunh? Use to be boys round where I come from they folks give em names like that."

"Where you from?"

"Arkansas. I went to school with a boy name JW, think it was, and he use to get real hot about it when people ask him what it stand for. It took me a long time to find out the reason why colored people put names like that on they children."

"Will you please tell *me.*"

"Should I tell him, Champ?" She winked at him and hunched him playfully with her elbow.

"I know how come you got names like that," Shakes broke out. "They cant think up nothin and finally just drop anything on the cat to make it sound like he got a name. Better than nothin, aint it, MC?"

Claire laughed and said, "Nope, that's not why. I dont feel like talkin and jivin with yall now. I got other things to do." She turned and started off but stopped and looked back. "But, MC, if you really wanna find out just stop back by sometime and maybe if I'm not too busy I'll run it down to you."

She switched off, leaving only a fragrance.

I felt put down and absolutely dumb.

Shakes said, "I do believe that broad go for you, MC."

Champ said, "I know she do. See, man, like I say—you hang in with me and we'll get everything taken care of. Let's get blasted!"

To get blasted you stood around and stood around and sat or leaned against the wall or the sink or the stove passing a joint around, sucking hard when it came your way and holding the smoke in by any means necessary. Grass was scarce and therefore expensive apparently because Champ kept stressing the importance of not losing any of the smoke.

"Keep it in, MC, dont care what happen, just keep holdin it in. Aint yall high yet? You mean you dont feel *nothin?* We been smokin on this gangster for a hour look like. Do *this!*" He took a puff and pinched his nostrils shut with his fingers and then blew into them without letting anything escape. "That's what you call frenchin and thatll usually get anybody straight right quick. Do it hard! Hold it in, MC, you lettin some out!"

"Damn, I cant hardly even breathe, Champ," I told him in that keen flat airless pot voice.

It got down to where we seemed to be passing around nothing more than a red-hot ash, thumping it at one another.

Both Shakes and Champ knew I had never smoked before and were determined to get me loaded. One joint went around. Two joints—and finally the third. "You mean to tell me you still dont feel nothin, MC?" Shakes said. "You jivin, nigger!"

I still wasn't sure but Champ and Shakes began laughing at me as I was licking my dry lips and wiping my mouth with my hand. "What's so damn funny?"

"You high yet, MC?"

"I dont know." I was dazed. "I dont know what I am."

"Then how come you keep lickin your lips," Champ wanted to know, almost in tears with laughter.

"Your mouth dry, MC?"

"Feel somethin like cotton, dont it?"

I let the last puff of smoke trickle out my nose and looked around for someplace to sit. Champ and Shakes continued to cut up at my expense. "What the hell is so funny? Do I look weird or somethin?"

"Just listen at the dude—'Do I look weird or somethin'—shoot, you look like you always do, like a cross between a chipmunk and a raccoon or maybe a beaver, what you think, Champ?"

"I always thought he kinda favored a Great Dane myself, round the jaws."

Even I had to give in on this one. Suddenly I was very conscious of my own physiognomy, not as something to be ashamed of—but the simple fact that people did look a certain way was mildly overwhelming. I sat in a chair, grinning uncontrollably. Shakes looked to me like a reddish furry creature of some kind himself.

"Would you say the dude was stoned?" Champ asked Shakes.

"Stoned *back!*"

Their very voices sounded strange, different, theatrical, like something someone had made up. I could feel my heart thumping and thought they heard it too. "Kinda loud, aint it?"

"What?"

"My heart, cant yall hear it too?"

Shakes cracked up and said, "Remember that story they put on us in lit class about The Telltale Heart, remember that? Who was it wrote that mess? Yeah, I know, Edgar Allan Poe, right?"

Already I felt a prolonged laughing spasm coming on.

Champ blinked at Shakes in slow motion, extinguishing the last of the joint between his fingertips and twisting all three butts into the end of a regular cigarette from which tobacco had been removed. "Anyone for cocktails?"

"That's what MC look like and it just now occurred to me—dude look like The Telltale Heart or The Raven or somebody. Dont he? Look at him close, round the eyes, little beady eyes all drawn up and red and the rest of him all shiny and black and slick-lookin. That's what The Raven look like."

Champ looked puzzled. "Raven? What old goddamn raven?"

"Aw, man, it's just some jive they had us studyin last semester at school. Quoth the raven nevermore, quoth the raven nevermore, knockin, knockin at my chamber door, hee hee hee hee—shit like that."

"O yeah," groaned Champ, "seem like I do remember somethin like that from someplace—some old weird motherfucker that use to write all that scary-ass shit, stories and things, wrote one bout this chump that fell off down in a pit or somethin, some funnytime stuff, man. Whew! I was half sleep at the back of the class when they was talkin bout that jive and the teacher call my name and ask me somethin and it look like I'd been dreamin all that stuff. Edgar Allan Poe, that's right! That's the dude use to stay half-juiced all the time, right? They tried to put me thru that litterchur shit two three times but I never could get it straight. I got to give the cat credit tho for that one thing he put out—that story bout that dude fell off down a ditch and they was gon crush his ass with that big-ass ball was swingin back and forth. That's one story shook me up for a long time. I had nightmares behind that shit, man. Fact, I still get halfway scared just thinkin about it. Let's talk about somethin else. Let's put on some sounds while we got our heads nice, before them broads get back and put our butts out. I know they got some tough sides round here cause I went out and copped a lot of em with my own two hands."

When I rose to go into the next room, I didn't so much walk as float.

"Hey, MC, feel like you could fly, dont you? Champ, I know MC got to be high cause I was blasted after my first toke and he done hogged up most of the pot. We better watch him right close."

"C'mon, man, I've been high before. I have a little taste every now and then."

"Naw, you cant jive the jiver, I aint goin for that," Shakes said. "You talkin bout bein drunk and I'm talkin bout bein high."

I was glad when we got to the livingroom and sat down in nice soft chairs. It seemed to have taken us forever to get there.

Music was very beautiful indeed. For the first

time, I felt as though I might be hearing things from Champ's angle, with his intoxicated ear, the way he had told me about in swim class that time. There were some drawbacks however.

Normally music to me was more than sound; it was a substance, something that not only filled my ear but that I could touch as well, a rolling, almost visible substance like technicolor fog puffed into a room, each sound having its own particular texture and effect on my nervous system. I could feel brasses; they were hard or soft, warm or cool. Some sounds were liquids, others solids, and other gases; reds, yellows, greens, earth browns, collapsible blues. When I read in books or heard musicians talk about eating, sleeping and breathing music, I felt I knew what they were talking about.

But under marijuana, I experienced something fresh in my listening, or so it seemed at first. Music disappeared. I mean, after Champ played the first track of a very quiet jazz LP and then tole me what he'd played, I couldn't believe that I'd actually listened to any music at all. I had blended completely into the music; I *was* the music and the whole story that the vibes, the piano, the bass and drums had told.

It was fun for a while but as we sat around in the half-dark listening to a band here, a band there, singers, fantastic soloists playing out of joy or crying out in pain, I also experienced a flash that made me feel that as exciting as it might have been to be listening to music high I still wasnt the person I usually was. It wasnt me doing the listening but someone else. It wasnt a comfortable feeling.

"This trumpet player sound like he comin down with the hiccups, dont he?" Champ said, and we all broke up, methodically, ritually.

I made it home all right that night, head full of strange angles, Claire, the smell of her still fresh in my melting brain, an intense and beautiful throbbing at the back of my head—

John Coltrane.

FIVE

THE NEXT DAY I wrote *Snakes.*

I should say: The next day I woke up with snatches of some melody skipping thru my head that I didnt know how to put together.

Everything was there, all the elements, but tying it all together was a feeling left over from a dream I'd had that night.

In the dream I was at a party. The people at the party were all people I knew well, people from school mostly—Champ, Shakes, Shakes' current girlfriend and another girl who hovered around the bandstand who was a perfect blend of Donna Lee Jackson and Claire.

Shakes and I were playing in a band that glowed

from the stands. I had full control of guitar and he had full control of drums. Flowers and the blue from some sky shimmered mistily against the surface of a shiny overlay that I seemed to be viewing the dream thru. The smell of the flowers, perfume and pot was everywhere. Every now and then the whole room, the whole building would do a little bounce. Somehow we'd coordinate our notes and accented chords to happen the same time as the bounce, the dip of the room. The beautiful dancers, who tacked on just the right flourishes with a wave of hands, were all moving in perfect time, the graceful ankles of black, brown and white chicks twisting and turning in the filtered colored light. While I played I was watching that concoction of Donna Lee/Claire and building my solo on her movements.

We were playing some funnytime hop music that had parts that sounded like water plopping. A kind of electricity crackled from everything the musicians were doing.

Donna Lee/Claire hovered specifically above me, finally, her head only, face poised in a sweet look that told me everything. Lips quivered down and kissed my ear. I responded by touching a warm note and holding it and waiting.

She became a whole body, and, surrounded by light, danced the perfect dance, her structure filling the room, blocking out everyone else. I lost track after that, so easily, so effortlessly.

I wanted to say something meaningful to Donna Lee/Claire but could think of nothing that I hadnt already said musically.

The tune that ran throughout the dream was what I woke up with, except that, somewhere along the line, somewhere between sleep and wakefulness, it had gotten jiggled into a jumble of phrases, ideas, fragments.

Now here Claude was at the morni[illegible]le asking me about my dreams. "What you [illegible]n last night, MC?"

"Dreamed about partyin."

"What you mean *partyin?* You mean you was at a *party,* you *met* somebody, somebody threw a *party* for you, or what?"

"All of em!"

"Hmmmmph! Sound like that might be that old party row. Lemme see, what number is that? Where my dreambook?" Into the drawer by the kitchen table she went. That's where she kept all of her numbers paraphernalia—slips, pencils, tipsheets, notebook from the dimestore for working out hunches, and, of course, the dreambook which is essential to the devoted numbers player.

Jezzy would be coming in just a little while.

I still felt a little funny from the night before but I was determined to work that melody out of it took me all day. All morning long, throwing papers, I had been trying to get it together.

Jezzy arrived as she always did, before I finished breakfast, before Claude got off to work. Jezzy was the route man, I guess you could say, the numbers runner.

Talk about your crazy people—I sat there that morning, still a little high, I believe, breakfasting on grits and eggs, and feeling as if I were watching a play take place in a theater. It was true domestic theater.

JEZZY (*lighting one up off of Claude's cigarette*): Girl, I just about had to jump on that m[illegible]d get him blessed good he got to worr[illegible]me so.
CLAUDE: What he do that's got you down on him so bad?
JEZZY: He wouldnt quit messin with me! Everywhere I'd go I'd look up and there he was, or else he'd be done gone and put one of his old good-for-nothin friends up to slippin in behind me and reportin back to him all what I was doin, what I was sayin. Now, how you gon deal with somebody carry on like that? Unh-unh, honey, I know from way back that it dont pay to be doin no type of business with nobody call theyself likin you.
CLAUDE: Is that what all that mess was about?
JEZZY: Yes, darling—that old nigger actually call hisself sweet on me, and he was determined not to let me make a dime, he wasnt gon let me make nary nickel he didnt know about!
CLAUDE: Well then, I cant blame you, but it's hard for me to believe that after all that time you been workin for him he didnt trust you no more than that.
JEZZY: Thought I was holdin out on him, girl, and all I can figger is one of them old low-down friends of his musta done told him I was holdin out on the pickup money—which

I was, but honest, Claude, it didnt amount to more than five or ten dollars a day at the very most. And them was tips I was gettin, the people was givin to *me, Jezzy!* But do you know that that man expected me to get up offa my little tips and split em with him!

CLAUDE: What was wrong with the man?

JEZZY: You know the answer to that just as well as I do. The man was crazy, that's all. Philly didnt have what I call good sense.

CLAUDE: Come to think of it, the two or three times me and Bo ran into him out there at Bunky Hutchinson's place on 8-Mile Road he didnt really act like he was all there, but me and Bo just figgered maybe he liked to drink and cut the fool like all them other old sorry-lookin Negroes like to hang out out there.

JEZZY: Noooo, Claude, Philly was just naturally crazy. He wasnt no half crazy or no three-fourths crazy. That man was one hundred percent pure dee insane, and then too because he was from outta Philadelphia and 'd done been in New York he kinda thought he was slick. Them eastern niggers is like that. They think it aint nobody that's got any sense but them. But he didnt know I could almost see clean thru his head and see his mind workin right while he'd be talkin to me—just like one of them old X-ray machines, that's how hip I was to what he thought he was puttin down.

CLAUDE: What was he puttin down, Jezzy?

Jezzy: Nothin! Wasnt puttin down a thing with that old rooster-lookin mouth of his.
Claude: What kinda mouth is that?
Jezzy: You know how old Philly's mouth kinda hang out from the rest of his face and his lips come to a point round the middle and them big old buck teeth of his with that gap get to snappin up and down like a woodchuck—and then, look here, when he go to talkin he kinda rear back and go to bobbin his head up and down and snappin them teeth and jeckin his finger round in your face and clickin his tongue. Hunh! I dont know what you think he look like but to me he favor one of them old roosters they use to have backhome raise a whole lotta sand round the barnyard ever time you look around.
Claude *(her head down on the table by now, her eyes streaming tears of laughter)*: Stop, girl, stop, you gon make me hurt myself! Tell me—tell me, what happen?
Jezzy: What you think happen? You dont see me workin for him no more, do you? I cut him aloose, that's what happen. I told him, I say, look here, Mr. Philly—
Claude: *Mr.* Philly?
Jezzy *(trying to keep a straight face)*: Yeah, *Mr.* Philly! I say, Look, baby, I know you think just cause you suppose to be a big eastern spender and I'm a Detroit Negro outta Georgia, I'm not suppose to be all that hip, but I'mo tell you somethin—I cant be your woman and your fool too, that just aint where

it's at, as the jitterbugs say. I am not here to play games. I am here to make a livin. Jezzy is strictly here on business, Mr. Philly, and I do not intend to get messed around. I make it a point to stay away from games that I do not like the way they run, and if I dont like the game I do not put on the suit because I am a grown woman and I have no intention of bein put in nobody's trick!

CLAUDE: What he say after that?

JEZZY: What could he say?

CLAUDE: You sure did tell him, girl!

JEZZY: Did I get him told?

CLAUDE: You blessed him out quite righteously!

JEZZY: Didnt I, didnt I?

This was the kind of dialogue they could keep up for hours and only brought to a close because each of them had to be on their way. Jezzy would check her watch and realize that if she didnt leave at that very moment, something terrible was liable to happen. This particular morning she peeped out the front window to make sure there were no police cars or suspicious-looking characters prowling about who could be taken for plainclothesmen. Once in a while she'd get picked up by the law but theyd have to release her when they were unable to find numbers slips or any other evidence of her occupation on her person or in her automobile. She said, "Got to be careful, you know. I aint got time to be sittin up in no jail, Claude. I got business to take care of. The man he got his business to take care of and I got mine. I cant be out here wastin time playin cops and robbers and carryin on. I dont mind so much bein picked up by these peckerwoods and things cause if they say one word to me and it strike me the wrong way I'll tell em to kiss my black ass in a minute! But these old splib cops, they think they slick. They be tryna sneak up on you like some kinda True Detective mystery or James Bond or somebody and they gets on my nerves sure enough! Wanna take you down and get credit and have the white man pat em on the head. I told one of em, said, Officer, while you detainin me it's people out here robbin and killin one nother." She put Claude's numbers away in a secret pocket of the big German lodencoat draped over her arm. "How you doin, MC? Youll be gettin outta school soon, wont you?"

"Ive got a little ways to go, but not much."

"That's good, you get yourself an education and then what you know they cant knock it out of you, and maybe you wont have to end up like poor old me and your grandmother here havin to be duckin and dodgin and easin by on the humble just to get a coupla dollars together. I'm *so* tired, and I *don't* intend to be fattenin no more frogs for snakes."

Five seconds after she got past that door, you could look out the window and up and down the street and she would be nowhere in sight—gone!

SIX

IT SEEMS odd to me that *Snakes* should have turned out to be one of our strongest numbers, *the* number, in fact, when you consider that Shakes and I must have written something like seventy-five songs that year, most of them variations on blues changes, to be sure; simple tunes that emphasized certain rhythmic ideas we were experimenting with at the time. We borrowed freely from jazz but were mainly concerned with working up a solid rhythm and blues setting to build a band around, a band that people could relax and dance to. There were gigs to be had around town and we saw no reason why we shouldnt be getting some of them.

Shakes was at the point where he could practically do what he wanted to do on drums, and I felt more confident than ever about my own playing. I was involved with the instrument to the extent of sitting in class or in study hall imagining runs when I should have been studying; working out fingerings in my head, and even forming my fingers, like Champ, around make-believe air guitars, tapping out patterns on desks and tables.

I loved *Snakes* though. The title sounded weird to some of the people we knew but the title was very important. The idea for it had come to me from a number of places but most notably from the expression *fattening frogs for snakes* that I'd heard Jezzy and Claude use a thousand times. Also, the melody itself was made up of tricky lines that to me sounded snake-like. The tune sounded simple the first time you heard it but it wasnt all that simple to play.

We knew we had a good thing going but it wasnt easy getting a band together. We worked out with quite a few bass and piano players before coming up with Jimmy Monday and Billy Sanchez. Jimmy was an easygoing kind of a guy who smoked a pipe and worked on cars when he wasnt playing bass. He had an uncle named Joe, Joe Monday, who played piano and led a small combo around town that made records for local consumption and that worked fairly regularly. Jimmy had done a lot of playing in school bands since junior high and in church, so he was solid and adaptable and had a feel for what we were trying to do. Billy Sanchez was a little older than the rest of us, a blind pianist who doubled on organ and who had been out of school for a couple of years. They were both very tough on their instruments and bent on developing their abilities, especially Billy who had been into jazz much longer than either Shakes or myself. They were also quiet guys who saw the commercial possibility of the kind of band we were trying to organize and knew when to hang loose and when to get business-like.

When we werent rehearsing nights in Shakes' basement, we'd be out in Billy's heated garage which was where he'd been doing most of his practicing for years. His folks had had it fixed up quite nicely for that, and it was where he spent most of his time.

We got up a pretty good repertoire, a book of some thirty or so pieces, solid numbers that included many of the hits of the moment that most local bands really have to have down. But we had quite a few originals too and the book was steadily growing, thanks to contributions by Billy who was forever pushing ahead of the rest of us in terms of ideas and trying out new things. Even then I felt he was doing us a favor by consenting to fool around with us, but Billy always did have that heart of gold.

Now and again Champ would stumble by and catch us painfully working our way thru a few things but he had gotten on a different kick lately, not having reenrolled in school that fall, and didnt seem to have much time anymore to be jiving with youngsters. He gave his approval and blessings to the band which we dubbed the Masters of Ceremony—because of my name, I suppose—but that was about it. "Yall sound goooood and you into a sweet little thing, mmmm, keep it up, keep it up—I got to run round here and get a coupla things together myself, check with you later, unh-hunh."

For the first time in my life I was feeling happy, very happy. I turned up at classes, faked my way thru, day-dreamed and planned things, my mind on music all the while, looking forward to our evening rehearsal, tingling. I was cheerful and popping, grinning in people's faces, and feeling at last that I was into something. That messy, uneasy feeling that I'd carried around inside me from as far back as I could remember broke up and gave way to a new sense of energy, endless energy.

Finally we felt that we were together enough to try the band out in public. Jimmy Monday and Shakes, since they had connections with the regular school band, managed to get us a twenty-minute guest slot at one of the Friday night post-basketball-game dances in the school gymnasium. It took some maneuvering on their part because Mr. Lied, the band and orchestra teacher, made it perfectly clear that he had little use for any musicians not directly involved with the school's official musical curriculum.

Ah, but we got on anyway, did a few of our popular numbers and ended up with a six-minute version of *Snakes*.

I was in my glory up there on the stand, not quite like in the dream but doing all right; cool, but so wrapped up in what the band was doing that I really didnt get much of a chance to watch the dancers and see how people were reacting to our music. As it turned out, we had everything so well under control that even when my high E-string snapped, as it had during many a rehearsal, I was still able to bring my part of the performance off without any hassle or real sense of crisis. I did, however, manage to get a glimpse of Donna Lee Jackson dancing with one of the guys from the regular dance band and smiling my way whenever she thought I might be noticing. She even sat one of the numbers out just to stand around and dig the band. This made me feel so good that I made up my mind then and there to hit on her the very next chance I got.

Members of the school dance band came up afterwards and congratulated us. It was obvious that some of them were jealous even though they tried to hide it.

Mr. Lied himself said, "You boys get an interesting sound, very interesting. Very good beat. You have a good drummer, of course, he's very accurate, and Jimmy here is a talented bass player. But there were places where I felt you could have used more rehearsal and where a bit more formal technique might have helped. But on the whole—very interesting."

Had Mr. Lied been the only listener on the scene that night, we might have come away mildly depressed, but there were all those other kids our own age who understood what we were putting down and showed us so by the way they responded.

Guys who never even spoke to me before came over and said things like, "Didnt know you played anything, MC. Hope you keep on, you guys were pretty good, better than the regular band, especially on that last thing you did."

"Didnt I tell you we was gon strike it rich?" Shakes said as we were packing up.

"I got about forty-five cents in my pocket, how much you got?"

"I got a dollar," Jimmy answered.

"That's all right," Shakes said, "this will prove to have been merely the beginning of something very diggable, gents."

SEVEN

WHAT DIED in me that night was any doubt that I might have had about our own ability, Shakes and mine, Jimmy's and Billy's. I lay awake in my room thinking about a hundred things, one right after the other, and over and over. I thought of my mother and father and wondered what they would make of me if they could see me now—funny-looking, going on 17, hung up on sounds, intense, virgin, ridiculous, lonely, wanting to belong.

What a mess I seemed to myself—no interest to speak of in sports or cars, no muscles, barely a mustache, no vices to speak of, no brothers, no sisters, not even a chick to hide my occasional pimples from. I had a dumb paper route that I was getting too old for, a few paperback books that I knew by heart, a well-used library card, a few well-worn records, a drawerful of sheet music, a guitar and raggedy amplifier upon which I could make a few runs, a few changes; a couple of buddies with whom I shared some interests and enthusiasms, and a grandmother who loved me almost more than I could stand, who fixed me meals and kept her eye on me and worked so hard, too hard, for me.

Was I lucky or stupid?

I couldnt decide.

I thought alternately of Donna Lee and Claire. Sweet Donna Lee who had made me feel worthwhile that evening. Thin, shapely Claire who knew even less about me than Donna. "Such is the simplicity of man to hearken after the flesh," Shakes always said, quoting his namesake.

The moon shone into my dirty window.

I loved the moon.

I loved everything a little bit more.

I wanted to hold some girl or woman and kiss her and lie with her until it was light.

I, I, I, I—who the hell was I?

Claude coughed and grunted, turning in her sleep in her stuffy room down the hall.

The people next door's dog let out a couple of yaps.

The streetcleaning trucks swished by in what sounded to me like three-quarter time, and I welcomed it for washing me away from my own silly cares. When it was gone, the cricket rhythms took the night back over, and I turned on my side and jacked off.

EIGHT

"DONT GO CRAZY!" Claude warned me when she became concerned that I was spending too much time practicing alone in my room or over at Shakes' and Billy's with the group. "These musicians and things, you gotta be careful. You all the time hear bout where one of em done gone crazy and lost they mind or got on that dope. Dont *you* go and go crazy on me, hear? I know you think you grown now and dont have to pay no attention to your old grandmama but I know what's best for you and I wouldnt lead you wrong. You keep keepin company with Chimp and them and next thing you know youll be on that dope and when you get on that stuff you might as well forget it!"

Claude was on one of her rampages. My plan was to patiently see her thru until she cooled down. I listened with one ear as I thumbed thru a copy of *Playboy*.

"You mannish rascal you! You gettin to be bout as mannish as that old simple-minded frienda yours, that Shakes. He so mannish till I cant hardly stand him no more, come up here to the door the other night askin for you and so mannish till I could smell him, smell like a goat or a sack of worms or somethin. I hope you know what you doin, MC. Poor thing. You didnt have no real mama or papa to bring you up decent, but I done the best I can. Do you think I done that bad a job of bringin you up?"

"C'mon, Claude, just because I'm readin this magazine . . ."

"Readin nothin! You was studyin that woman's body, I was lookin dead at you, you cant fool me! I'm the one raised you, remember?"

"What harm is it to look at a picture of somebody in a magazine?"

"Some*body* is right, I should smile—just dont go tryna put anything over on me, child. I know you."

"At least I'm not out rapin anybody or anything like that."

"Better *not* be! And dont come gettin smart with me, boy. You might be bigger than me but I'll still reach over and pop you one—pick up this tablespoon and bop you right in your devilish mouth!" She sat down in a chair and sighed. "MC, I would so much like for you to go on thru school and make somethin outta yourself. You speak well. You read a lot. You seem to have the intelligence. I even enjoy your music, what little I can understand, only I wish yall wouldnt play it so loud sometime. You have the ability to make anything out of your life you want to. You could go on to college, go right up here to Wayne State and study to be a lawyer. I think youd make a good lawyer because you can just naturally talk—when you feel like it. You could be a teacher or an accountant or anything you choose. You have the brains, but look like to me all you wanna do lately is run around with these old so-called hip niggers, these little jitterbugs. And that's all they are is jitterbugs. You got too much on the ball to be throwin your life away like that."

"But what have I done that's wrong, just tell me what's wrong with what Ive been doin?"

"You stay out too late at night and that aint good. You come in wakin me up and I look at the clock and it be almost two o'clock in the mornin sometime, and on the weekend you come in even later than that."

"It's kids at school that stay out a whole lot later than I do."

"I'm not talkin about them, I'm talkin about you."

"I get my route done and I keep up in school, dont I?"

"Maybe so, but that isnt the point. You got to do better!"

"Better than what? You used an adjective of comparison, and–"

"Now, dont go throwin that stuff they taught you in school up in my face. I dont stand correctin. You know what I'm talkin bout. Your mother was smart, sharp as a tack when it came to book learnin. I always thought she was gon up and make somethin outta *her*self."

"Now, there you go getting on Flo again. As far as I'm concerned, she was beautiful, and my daddy was beautiful. They couldnt help what happened to them."

Claude's face slackened when I said that. She

reached across the table and touched my hand, squeezed it gently. "I'm sorry, MC. You know I would be the last one to say anything bad against my own daughter. I just want you to stop and take a look at yourself. All you seem to really care about is playin that guitar and bein in music."

"So what's wrong with that?"

"Aint nothin the matter with it, dont get me wrong. You *are* doin a whole lot better'n a lotta these children out here they folks brung em here into the world, and they just lost. Children nowdays just seem to be lost. They lost, they folks is lost. I raised you and I love you and I want you to amount to somethin."

"So I wanna be somethin, I wanna be a musician."

"If that's what you wanna be, then why dont you do it right? Why dont you go on to college and study music?"

"The way I'm doin it is right for me. I play. I taught myself to play and write music."

"Your uncle downsouth taught you how to play. You mean you done forgot them first lessons he gave you?"

"All right, all right, but I developed it myself. I'm studyin all the time on my own. You seem to think just because I'm not takin formal lessons in music that I'm not really serious about it."

"No, no, it isnt that. What I'm scared bout is you might be a little *too* serious about it. I dont want you to get in no trouble. You might not think it, but I know a little somethin bout music and musicians too, the kind you seem to wanna be, the kind that play all that blues and stuff. It aint no life, believe me. You scuffle and work in these old smoky nightclubs playin for drunk people, and you take up with these slummy women that be's all mixed-up, poor things, all they know is to get in behind some pitiful musician. You drink that whiskey and smoke anything anybody hand you and next thing you know—"

"I already know what youre goin to say: You start usin narcotics."

"That's right—that old dope, and then you dont do nothin but go from sugar to shit, if youll excuse my French."

"Well, I wish youd wait until I do somethin that you can get on me about before you start lightin into me."

"Then itll be too late. You dont seem to understand, child. I'm not that worried about you really. I just wouldnt want you to get yourself hurt before you find out what this world is all about. Youd be surprised to know what this hard, cold, iron-hearted world is all about, sweetheart. And you black too! It aint gon be easy. Me, I messed up. Your mama and daddy they got off on the wrong foot and the Lord for some reason taken them on way from here. I want you to make it."

"Claude, I'll make it."

"I sure hope so."

"Can I go now?"

"Where to?"

"Back to this article I was readin."

"OK, Mr. Big, you know what you doin."

Later that evening as I was packing my guitar to go practice, she called to me.

"Yes, ma'am!"

"Why dont you stay home tonight?"

"What for? There's nothin goin on around here. I need to get in a solid night of practicin with the guys."

"The guys, the guys! That's all I ever hear bout is the guys, the band! Dont it ever occur to you I might like you to be round here with me at home sometime? Why dont you stay home for a change? We can watch television and talk with one another."

"I would, Claude, but you dont understand. We're gonna be getting jobs soon workin dances and we've got to work some things out. We may even be goin on television ourselves soon."

"Yall?"

"That's right."

"What program yall gon be on?"

"We sent in to that *Stars to Come* show for an audition."

"I'll be! You mean that band yall got? Well, I'll just be! More power to you."

"Goodnight, Claude." I kissed her on the forehead. "I do appreciate you."

"Yeah I know bout how much you preciate me. Just be careful."

"Of what?"

"Everything—your friends, your girlfriends, everything."

"Claude . . ."

"I'mo pray for you, hear?"

NINE

It's a windy night some time later. It's fall in the City of Motors, the smell of gasolines and oils everywhere; dust, smog, exhaust pipe farts. Soot merges with dust and dust merges with darkness. In my changeless room I run the calluses of my fingertips over the neck of my guitar until I cant stand it anymore.

Records are a drag. What are they anyway but reminders, a record of something that once was and can never be again in the same way—like those photographs of my grandmother's.

Music is only sound after all and where would I be if I didnt know that?

Champ's out someplace. Who knows where? I havent seen him in weeks.

Shakes is probably laid up with one of his mythical lovelies, doing that thing.

Ive been frittering the evening away on sticky, stupid apéritif wine, they call it, a bottle of Thunderbird left here by Champ long ago. A phrase in my head makes me giggle: "A sweet taste of Bird to unstick my wings, man"—Is this what blues is?

MC, I says, offering myself another gulp and accepting it, Shakes was right. You never do anything adventurous. Not even recreational. You never even do anything necessary. Go on out and do something for a change!

I dress in my best trousers and coat and make it out the door without being asked anything, down the block to where there aint no guitar, aint no recordplayer, no band to rehearse, no nothing but pure music, uncut, uncomposed—just solid sound, everywhere.

Just the music of black people moving every whichway: dudes, chicks, little children who should be home digging on the video cowboys, ridiculous cops driving up and down, around and around. I remember nights when we lived—Bo, Claude and me—on Beaubian Street on the east side and I'd be laid down to sleep nights in my project bed that my guardians and the state provided me with, fast by my pillow, listening to the Big Four (a notorious quartet of brutal policemen who prowled the streets and alleys in sedans looking and asking for nothing but trouble) beating the shit out of someone in the alley behind our place. That poor victim, poor man, would cry out when they hit him, and I, in my bed and pajamas, would cry along with him and tremble. I can picture it all so clearly, center it in my mind, see them stopping him on a corner and pushing him hands down against the fender of a car as they search him, humiliate him, put him thru those frightening changes, their cold hands hovering over strapped-on pistols. Theyd stop a blind man. Theyd stop Billy Sanchez, a religious and devout musician, make him take off his shades and shine high-powered flashlights into his wounded blank eyes.

Loaded on Bird by now, I wobbled carefully down 12th to the brownstone building on Euclid where I knew Claire was.

Knock knock.

"Who is it?"

"MC."

"MC?"

"Yes, *me*. You know?"

She was alone. It was an anonymous Tuesday school night. Both the other chicks, Leona and Michele, must have been out laying down hustles. Claire looked at me hard thru the slit in the door before sliding the latch back. "O, *you!*"

"That's what I said—*me*. Remember you told me to drop back by sometime if I wanted to find out how come a lotta people give their kids initials for names?"

"O yes, baby, how could I ever forget you? Youre a frienda Champ's, aint you? Yall came by here that night I was on my way out. You play the drums, right?"

"That's my friend plays drums. I'm the guitarist, MC, remember?"

"Of course, of course—MC. I remember that all right, thought it was the funniest name I'd heard in a long time. I dont mean to offend you or anything, but—come on in. My brother play guitar. Come on in."

I was nervous, naturally, but emboldened by wine and by images that had been plaguing me since the first time I'd seen her. There was a mirror on the wall near where we stood and I glanced at myself standing in the half-light beside an attractive young woman who couldnt have been more than three or four years older than myself.

She was all dressed up, slick-eyed, shiny-lipped, "Hope I'm not interruptin anything, Claire. Were you about to go out, or—"

"Aint no big thing. Sit down, sit down. You want anything? You wanna cigarette? You wanna drink?"

"No."

"No, what?"

"I dont want anything. I came to talk to you."

"Relax. What you wanna talk about?"

"Well . . . So you got a brother that plays guitar, hunh?"

"Now, come on, baby—you didnt come all the way up here to talk about my brother."

Off the wall. I felt about as off the wall as they came—half-drunk, half-scared. "Claire—"

"That's my name."

"Claire, you said if I ever wanted to know why people put names like MC on kids—"

"—to come on back round here sometime, yeah. You really wanna know how come?" She got a cigarette out and sat on the couch next to me, feet curled up beneath her. "Well. It's because a long time ago back in the south they use to wouldnt call colored people except by their first names. You could be workin right longside a cracker for thirty-five years and the boss'd still call *him* by his last name—'C'mere, Carter, and let's have a talk!' —or either if he was really in tight with the big-shots theyd call him by his initals—'Well now, JW, if you ask me, I think we should'—are you followin me? So then a few black folks started gettin hip and gave their children names like Wilson or Spaulding or Lincoln, last names first, you dig it, or either put names on them like CW or LC or, heh, MC so that even if they never managed to get into any important positions, theyd still sound like they was important. So, like, when the man called your name out, it sounded like you had some status anyway, whether you did or not. You knew the man wasnt gon call you by your last name like he would another honky, not them peckerwoods back in those days. Now. Does that satisfy your curiosity, MC?"

I felt so silly that I almost got up and left. "Thank you. That's been on my mind, you know, ever since that night."

"How old are you, MC?"

"Nineteen."

"You aint no nineteen and you know it! Bet you anything you aint a day over seventeen—if you that old. Do you have a girlfriend?"

I sat there drunk, like a mannikin, only breathing, breathing hard. "Well, not at the moment. I broke up with the last chick I was goin with."

"Broke up? What over?"

"She was kinda, you know—jive."

"Jive?"

"Yeah. She couldnt dig what I was into and went for all this old hippy-dippy shit and—"

"Aw, cut it out!"

"Beg your pardon."

"Cut it out. You dont have to be runnin all that down to me, especially since it isnt any of my business. Even if it was for real you should keep it to yourself. What exactly is it that you suppose to be into?"

I was tired of lying and pretending. "Not a hell of a lot, Claire." I was speaking to her eyes the way I thought it was supposed to be done. At least she didnt seem to be in any hurry to get rid of me. "No, I'm not into all that much. I love my music, and I do my thing, and–"

"Do you want some pussy?"

"Whew! You caught me by surprise with that one, baby. I–"

"Didnt you come up here to hit on me, or what?"

"Yeah–well–what can I say?"

"Just dont be wastin my time and your time with some old chickenshit hype about how old you are and who your girlfriend was and first one thing and another."

"Listen, Claire. I dont have that much bread on me. I dont know what you ask and all that, but I can–"

"Aw, shut up, nigger. If I wanted your money youda never got up here in the first place cause it's a whole lotta people out there in the street got more money than you gon see in a long time." She rose and smoothed the wrinkles from her skirt with her tiny hands. "MC, you crack me up."

We wound up in a little room. There was a cheap gooseneck lamp on a low table in there, bulb bent to the wall, a rug on the floor, a radiator, dresser, a picture of a little boy in a frame on the table next to the lamp, and the bed.

I stood in the middle of that little room feeling like a fool, wondering what I should do next. Should I kiss her? Should I slob on the broad, as the saying went? I thought of all the mouths that had slobbed and, no doubt, slobbered on hers, and I thought of all the tongues her tongue had touched and tasted.

She didnt say anything for a long time, but walked around gathering loose pieces of clothing from the bed and dresser and hanging them up in the closet. Then she carefully crushed her cigarette out in an ashtray and stood looking at herself in a mirror, this one a full-length mirror; looking at herself and at me who stood in back of her looking like Beetle Bailey. I was admiring her thin brown arms and the way they turned into shoulders; the little breasts beneath her lemon jersey, the graceful lines of her face and lipsticked mouth; the magazine teeth that emerged as she smiled, as her smile became a laugh.

"Are you laughin at me, Claire?"

"No."

"Youre pretty, you know."

"MC?"

"Yes."

"Help me undo my top."

"OK." I was shucking again, pretending that this was something I did every day, every night, when the only woman I'd ever even remotely helped with her clothing was Claude those rare instances when she got dressed up and asked me to zip the back of a dress or blouse for her, or fasten a couple of those worrisome snaps or hooks at the back of the neck.

She smelled sweet, but not too sweet and a little too human. Perfume mixes so strangely with sweat.

I unzipped her and stood around some more.

She did the rest, slipping out of her bra and pants but leaving the creamy slip on, easing herself down onto the edge of the bed, still smiling privately. What was she smiling at? At me? At the windowshade, at the picture of the child in the frame on the table, at the air between us in the room? "Come here. Sit down. Take your shoes off, MC. Unbutton your shirt. Unzip your pants. You can take em off while you at it. You dont know what a good thing you came up here and fell into. I dont ordinarily go thru all this for somebody when it's just me out there turnin another trick. This is special, nigger. You remember that."

She pressed her lips to my chest and got up. "Want me to turn the light out?"

"It doesnt bother me."

There was a little trojan I'd been carrying around in my wallet going on a year. Shakes had laid it on me. I went into my trousers and got it out. Claire lay back. I fumbled around getting the paper band off the white prophylactic. She sat up. "What's that you got there? Hey, lemme see!"

I wanted to hide. "Just this." I let her see.

"O, I see. I thought you was breakin out a joint. I was gon ask you to please turn me on!"

"No, sorry—it's just a prophylactic, a rubber."

She pulled me down. "You run your mouth too much. If you just learned to keep your damn mouth shut, youd be all right."

There was nothing I could say now, no words left in me, not even a whisper. All that groovy bullshit I'd been saving up to lay on her and now I couldnt say boo. If I could have said anything it would have been: What do I do now?

She rubbed me all over with her hands the way she'd smoothed those wrinkles from her skirt. I was so jive and petrified that, instead of getting bigger, I got smaller and smaller, smaller than I thought it was possible for me to get.

But she kept running her fingers and palms over me, touching, touching, trying to get that rise out of me. I was trying to retrieve all my recent fantasies, secret daydreams, bed dreams, ninety-second shorts in which we carried on something terrible with one another, me and Claire, me and Donna, me and Claire and Donna in a room, in the woods, in a basement, anywhere, nowhere, doing it, doing it, this way and that.

"I'm turning out the light," she whispered into my mouth and touched me with her teeth.

Darkness made the difference.

Everything disappeared.

We kissed and tussled.

I pulled the covers up over us.

That last gulp of wine caught up with me and my head began to vibrate inside.

She batted her eyelids against my shoulder, my cheek.

A police siren screamed down 12th, the wind, the hawk of that night trailing it.

I listened to my heart speeding up, and, awkward as a child or an old man, fiddled with her meat until she took charge softly and guided me home.

The door at the front of the apartment opened some time later. A man's and a woman's voice came seeping thru the keyhole and underneath our door.

For some strange reason, I relaxed instantly after that, knowing we werent exactly alone.

It was my first time holding a woman and I thought I had to say something. "Youre so soft, Claire."

"Shhhhhh . . ."

TEN

THE *Stars to Come* TV show did it.

I mean, we had it down! Everything came off perfectly. Our only complaint was with Shakes. He came off looking just a little too clownish for the rest of our tastes. The camera zoomed in and there he was, grinning and mugging to beat the band; literally doing everything short of breaking in a 1927 buck and wing. I flinched when they played the tape back for us at the studio. Jimmy

Monday—always the coolest member of the group and perfect example that there was such thing as reserve—said, "Damn, Shakes, I thought you were gonna go into some kind of Scat Man Curruthers routine any minute there. What the hell's the matter with you? It's only a television program, you know."

"I'se gwine ter tell yall all I knows about de niggers dat's plannin ter ekscape, Cap'n, suh, shonuff, yazzum," I threw in.

Luckily, Billy Sanchez couldnt see him.

Shakes didnt quite know what to do, how to react, finding himself being ridiculed so keenly. "Listen, fellas," he said, "I know what youre tryna tell me but I dont see it that way. I was just doing the best I knew how and that's how it came out. Nothin wrong with a little showmanship, is there? You dont have to treat me like I'm Kingfish or somebody."

Jimmy was really upset. "It's just that your clowning, throwing your sticks all up in the air and twirling them, was that necessary? It isnt so much you came on like Kingfish as it is you put the rest of us in that Mystic Knights of the Sea Lodge Hall bag."

"Look at that!" I said. "Check yourself out right now on that screen with that Rastus grin!"

There was nothing we could do about the tapes. We tried to talk the director into editing out the shots of Shakes for the telecast that coming Saturday, but he told us that we were fine, just fine, and he saw no reason to cut anything, adding confidentially that ours had been the liveliest "act" they had featured in a long time.

Well, it was a break, it was a beginning. People would see us, the show would go into so many homes that someone would have to notice us and give us a job. At least Donna Lee would be watching. I was going to see to that.

The show went on.

Our appearance on the *Stars to Come* show, besides bringing local recognition, brought us a number of prizes as well. The first week on, we all won wristwatches and cheap recordplayers. During the next semifinals week (at the end of each month they pitted all the weekly winners against on another), we each got television sets. Eventually, as we were brought back again and again, we finally beat out all the singers and acrobats and accordion players and copped the big grand prize—full four-year scholarships to the college (s) of our choice.

A man named Abdullah Salah sent a letter to the station asking if we had a manager, and the station turned the letter over to me.

ELEVEN

ABDULLAH SALAH had a wife named Rose and together they operated a recording firm called

Moonbeam Records. I had passed it many times since the building they operated out of wasnt far from school It was a strictly local label. Jimmy's uncle, Joe Monday, made records for them.

Joe played what was known as "funkybutt" blues. He played piano and was always backed by an excellent rhythm section. A number of musicians who, at one time or another, had worked for him as sidemen later turned up in New York and made big names for themselves on the national scene. Joe's records for Moonbeam were big sellers around the Detroit area as well as places like Toledo, Ohio and Gary, Indiana—solid working towns where people got their paychecks every Friday afternoon, lined up and cashed them, went home and got out of their workclothes, and hit the streets that very night to party and frolic in the clubs and joints until it's Sunday again. T-Bone Walker told the whole story in his *Stormy Monday Blues.*

"Yeah, I get offers to come over to New York and get in on the bigtime," Joe told us, "but I know where it's at, and where it's at is right here." He tapped at his head with a finger. "You got to be together up here these days. Why should I go over there and live like a dog when I can gig anytime I feel like it here in Big D? Pretty soon, I'll have me enough to quit drivin that old truck around during the week and can get my barbecue place underway. That's what I really wanna do. See, if you not too hip and you get in on that bigtime, so called, well, before you know it the gangsters'll be done moved in and hemmed you in on all four sides, then you got to do what they say do. Ive seen that happen to so many performers."

Because Jimmy was in the Masters of Ceremony, Joe took an interest in us and gave us a lot of good advice that I can appreciate now more than ever. He told us that Moonbeam wasnt a bad little label to record for and that we'd do all right with Abdullah, who was interested in recording us, so long as we didnt attract too big a following.

"That shouldnt be difficult," I told him jokingly.

"Well, youd be surprised, youngster, at how things go once they get out of your hands. When you put a record out you dont know who's gonna go for it, if it's the first time. Maybe people in a certain age bracket might go for it, maybe people in just one town. Maybe nobody. Maybe itll turn out a hit. You never know. Now, close as I can tell, Abdullah's pretty honest, as honest as they come in this business. Ive been with him goin on five years and the only complaints Ive got with him are so picayunish theyre not even worth mentionin. I switched over to Moonbeam from this other label on the eastside that I felt was messin me around. Moonbeam *will* stand behind and push you, you can count on that. Theyll even make a star outta you if that's what you want, but it takes time, takes a long time and a helluva lotta work. Me, I wouldnt be no star for nothin in the world, not even for five million dollars, as much as I love money. When you get up there, I mean really up there, it's so easy to lose touch with the people and with yourself and the kinds of things that made you what you are, know what I mean?

The way I play doesnt come from out here in Grosse Pointe, it comes from me, and I come from a whole lotta places. But Abdullah will push you if that's what you want. Theyll put your records out, get them played over the radio so people can hear them, like on Poppin Percy's Show and over that other colored station too, and even over the white stations sometime. He lines up gigs for us to play too. You kids got yourselves a sweet little tune, that *Snakes*. If you can come up with a half dozen more like that then you might be able to retire before youre thirty. In fact, I was thinkin of makin a version of it myself and, quite naturally, you all would get a little kickback, royalties for writin it. Hell, if your record starts gettin too big, Abdullah and Rosie they automatically turn it over to one of the big national companies. They almost had to do that with that number we had out a little while back, *Nasty Mustards*. Tell me it caught on all downsouth. We got a letter here the other day from some cat that runs a place down in Hee Haw, Louisiana wanted to know if we could come down and work a week."

"Well—we're just trying to get a start. We're not out to raise any sand but we would like some jobs so we could make a coupla dollars."

"Aw, youll do all right. I saw you on TV. Your drummer here really knows how to put on a show. People like that. I think white people like that more than they go for our music."

We all looked at Shakes who made an ugly face. "What's everybody lookin at me for?"

"I'm old," Joe said, "I'm a family man now and

gettin too old, so I have to do what's best for me and them both. You guys are youngsters—young, free and crazy and fulla energy, and energy is what it takes."

After talking it over with Joe and with our folks, we signed a contract with Moonbeam to do four sides, two singles with an option for them to issue an album if response seemed promising. Abdullah fixed us up with the musicians' union and gave us a hundred dollars apiece in advance, more money than any of us had ever had at one time.

I was scared.

TWELVE

OVER CHRISTMAS VACATION, while school was out, we took up residence at Moonbeam's dilapidated office and studio on Linwood Avenue, a few blocks from school. It was one of those killer Decembers. The hawk was talking! The worst cold of the season had blown in so fiercely that no one in his right mind would have even left the house. Not being in our right minds, we made daily trips to and from the studio. Shakes left his drums set up there.

The studio was nothing like those big, well-lighted, well-equipped recording studios I was to become acquainted with years later as a sideman.

Moonbeam occupied the quarters of what had once been a store of some kind, a large shop. Inside you walked thru a small front office crammed up with desk, typewriter, countless papers, posters, glossy 8 x 10s of Moonbeam artists (a huge one of Joe Monday) which is where Rosie Salah must have spent the better part of her wakeful hours talking on the telephone and jotting things down. She was a pleasant, chubby, middle-aged lady, frizzly-haired, who wore glasses that made her look owl-eyed. Curiously enough, she and her husband bore a remarkable resemblance to one another, both of them being short, sallow-complexioned, friendly and graying. They both dressed well but not stylishly; subdued, I thought, particularly when compared with some of the outlandish outfits their artists got themselves up in.

At the back of this closet office you came to a thick gray door with a message painted on it in bold black letters:

RECORDING
DO NOT ENTER WHEN RED LIGHT IS ON

We spent ten days and ten nights behind that door, Mr. Salah off to one side in a small glassed-off control room, clicking switches, marking tapes, blurting out directives and suggestions to us over the P.A.

We did *Snakes* the first night in three takes. We had only rehearsed it a thousand times.

Nine days later we had the other three tracks in the can, as they say.

It all seems to have been done by magic but, after all, we worked hard, very hard, getting things to sound just the way we wanted, and we wanted the band to sound good.

"What do you think?" I asked Mr. Salah.

"I think you fellows should go home and get some rest."

"Do you think we've got anything worthwhile?"

Mr. Salah was glowing. "MC, I dont think you have anything to worry about. In fact, if you can hold the group together, I'd say that we were all in for some better days ahead."

PART THREE

ONE

EVERYTHING HAPPENED so fast.

Claude didnt know what to make of any of it. "Well, at least you got a little money comin in and it look like this Mr. Salah is a man who keeps his word. It's hard to believe we got a few hundred dollars in the bank, MC. But what about your schoolin? You still got a semester to go. I do want you to finish up—but with all this record stuff, I dont know. I just dont know. The money's nice, I must admit that. I guess I just dont understand what's goin on."

"What's goin on, Claude, is we're gonna make it."

"We wasnt doin all that bad before."

"Maybe not, but isnt it nice to be able to look forward to a little extra money?"

"It isnt the money."

"Then what's bothering you now?"

She sat in a chair and began to cry. "I'm sorry, MC, I dont know what's the matter with me carryin on this way."

"Are you upset about somethin?"

"No, I dont think so, I dont know."

"Then please dont cry, Claude." I sat on the arm of the chair beside her. "I'll finish up school all right, dont worry about that. I wouldnt throw all that away. Besides, Ive been thinkin about usin that award we got from that TV show to go away to some school, some music school where I could study things like theory and harmony and composition. Those things're important to know if youre gonna go into music seriously."

"And what's gon become of your band while you off at college?"

I laughed, or, rather, forced a laugh. I placed my hand on her shoulder. "Now I get it!"

"Get what?"

"Now I think I understand what's been on your mind since our record came out and all the excitement's been goin on."

She wiped her eyes on the hem of her apron, but, sniffling, continued to keep that woeful expression, cutting one reddened eye my way. "MC, it's all right, it's all right, baby, you dont have to sit here with me. I just havent been feelin too good. I hate to cry in front of anybody, especially you."

"Mama"—I rarely called her that—"Mama, are you afraid I'm gonna go off and leave you here alone, by yourself?"

She wouldnt answer.

"Listen, Mama. Look at me. I wouldnt do that. Do you think I'd go and do somethin like that after all youve done for me? Youre all Ive got in this world—you and my music. I couldnt just walk off and leave you. Really, I couldnt. I wouldnt."

Again tears came rolling from her eyes in silence. She had always cried by herself in silence.

"MC, sweetnin, would you go get me some Kleenex?"

When I got back with the Kleenex, she had already dried her eyes again on the hem of the apron, but she took the tissue and used it to yawn into. "I dont mean to come apart like this but like I told you, I been worried about you. I dont know who you are anymore. Do that strike you as funny?"

"No, I think I understand."

"You always say that but do you really? I'm glad to see yall got a record out and people wantin to hear your numbers and like that but what I wanna know is what is it all leadin up to? Are yall gon quit school and get in with them show business people and go out on the road or just keep makin records round here in town, or what? I done lost track of you. You arent the same MC I knew. I'm glad to see you takin it all so calm tho, that's a good sign, but do you know really what you gettin into?"

"Yes, I know what I'm gettin into. It's nothin to be sad about, I know that much. All we're doin is cashin in on some of the hard work we've been puttin into our music, and we're not that big at all. We'll be lucky if we make a thousand dollars apiece all told before our record plays out—but we might can get some jobs and keep it goin awhile. Is that all that bad? Doesnt it beat playin the numbers? Listen, all my life Ive watched you slave and scrimp and put all your little extra money into those numbers. The numbers are a long shot. What I'm doin isnt much but it's a hell of a lot surer than–"

"So now youre old enough and so big and important that you can cuss in front of your grandmother, hunh?" She started to cry again.

"Claude, Mama, please dont cry. I'm just trying to tell you how I look at the thing. Playin's the only thing interests me for now, but I'll finish school first and then figger out what to do next. In the meantime, what's wrong with makin a coupla bucks?"

She got quiet for a long time, then she said, "If you went away to school, like you said you been thinkin bout doin, would you be satisfied to go up here to Wayne State or the Conservatory or would you wanna go away to some other state?"

"Wayne would be OK, I guess."

"You guess, hunh?"

"I havent decided yet, Claude, but no matter where I choose those TV sponsors'll pay for my tuition and books–it wont cost us that much."

She wiped her eyes and stood up. "I want you to be happy. Like I told you a hundred times, you got so much to offer and people that put out records're a dime a dozen. I want you to be happy. All my life I been wantin to see somebody happy. I never found it for myself except when I'm around the people I love. I aint exactly pitiful neither. I got me a fine grandson to be proud of and I probly shouldnt tell you this but I think you old enough to make up your own mind about things. You know what you wanna do. People do what they have to do. I left home when I was your age, *before* I was even your age. I know I'm old and square and dont know what's happenin but it would break my heart to see you unhappy. I'm prayin for you like I told you I would." She stretched herself and yawned again. It was way past her bedtime. "If only Bo had lived, then it woulda been a man round the house to deal with you. Your poor grandmother, any poor woman can only just do so much." She placed both hands on my head and looked at me hard with her wet eyes. She smelled of Noxema. "You see, MC, the point is that I love you."

I didnt have any answer to that one. I simply looked at her, feeling stupid.

"Child," she said, "I hope you dont think I'm meddlin again but look here—why dont you run round the corner here to Campbell's Barber Shop tomorrow and get some of this mess cut offa your head. You startin to favor the Wolf Man."

TWO

MR. SALAH DECIDED it might be a good idea to limit our personal appearances until school let out that coming June. Jimmy Monday, Shakes and I would be graduating if all went well. Billy Sanchez had nothing to worry about, having snared his H.S. degree several semesters back.

Snakes wasnt doing too badly as a single. That spring Moonbeam planned to release a whole album of us and book us up with as many gigs as we thought we could handle around the area. They said theyd even try to get us a spot in the Emancipation Proclamation ceremonies that were staged every summer across the river in Canada. We were put on salaries of fifty dollars a week in the meantime which was Mr. Salah's way of encouraging us to stay close to Moonbeam. Of course, for this, we were also expected to make local TV appearances to plug the record and to work occasional weekend jobs. But there was very little of the heavy kind of pressure to produce that I had been expecting and dreaded.

We didnt practice that much anymore. We were too busy. A couple of hours after school seemed to do the trick. Already I missed those exhausting sessions we used to have, the challenge of always striving to make a thing sound better, the good feeling among the musicians. Now when we got together we paid more attention to things like timing, how long a piece lasted and would it be a good number to record; what kind of monotonous bass figure Jimmy should play repeatedly throughout to help anchor the beat for the dancers; how short a drum break should be, and so forth. Our considerations were becoming primarily professional.

By now the whole pattern of my day was changing too. No longer having to get up mornings to go throw those papers, I sat up nights and goofed in my room, smoking secretly like an amateur nicotine fiend, and listening to the all-night jazz show, barely audible on my radio, from CKLW, Windsor. With the window cracked, even when it was snowing out, I paced the floor in my socks and jotted down ideas on musical score paper.

I also began keeping a diary that year, inspired by diaries and journals I'd checked out of the library. Every day I made entries like a tidy, dutiful rememberer of things, and crossed nothing out, even when what I wrote didnt seem to make sense. I wigged away many a night that way, unseen, alone. I knew the jazz people were into something but I wasnt sure what exactly. How exciting it would be, I thought, to be like those mysterious living musicians whose records came out on offbeat labels. Now I know that I was only beginning to undertake a kind of self-exploration that would drag on for years. For then, it was just fun; the era of mass hipness was yet to come, and I thought very little about the meaning of what I was doing. But today when I go back and read some of those diary notes, it helps me to see where I was at then.

10th February

Copy of our record before me as I scribble: flat circular object w/ large hole in center & bright yellow label specked w/ information—

Moonbeam
Lunar Music BMI Time 2:42
45 rpm
SNAKES
(M. C. Moore)
The Masters of Ceremony
10025

It's hard to believe that this little object has been duplicated thousands of times & packed & boxed & distributed all over the place & can be bought for a little over $1.00 by anyone who wants it & has the money to pay for it.

Will the Law of Diminishing Returns that we are learning about in Mr. Minton's econ class (I wouldn't mind diminishing him) take its toll upon our product?

I can't stand to listen to it anymore & only wish that the good people who hear it daily over such faithful programs as the Popping Percy Show could realize that it's just a little something that I literally dreamt up & was able to pull into listenable shape with the help of my constituents, James "Shakes" Harris, William Sanchez, & James Monday, Jr.

It's freezing out tonight and there's a brilliant circle around my old friend the moon.

Meantime, where is Champ? When will I ever get to talk with Donna Lee Jackson alone? Everybody at school likes us now & wants to be friends. Even the e-lites (the sons & daughters of colored professionals & other legalized hustlers), who wouldn't even look at me before because I was too dark and nappy-haired, invite us to their "affairs" & "functions" & I, like the moon, could care less.

Tomorrow night we work Soupy's Show on channel 7. Claude says she will watch. Billy Sanchez says he'll be watching too (he loves to make those weird jokes that blind people make the rest of us uncomfortable with). He's always offering to drive people home, etc. I should take him up on it.

One day I'm going to get me a guitar that you can plug earphones into & not have to disturb anyone else when you practice.

Meanwhile I smoke my Kools & listen to saxophones & flutes over the radio & think of Donna Lee who sits next to me now in English Comp.

23rd February

Doorbell rings while Claude's away & it's Champ at the door. I don't know what to do for him. He falls in w/ a painful grin & says he wants to use my bathroom & then stumbles in, clicks the door to & I can hear him moaning & throwing up in there & liquid plopping into liquid, coughing, hacking, terrible sounds. He comes out wiping his mouth w/ handkerchief, heads for my room, falls on the bed huffing & puffing, says he can't keep anything on his stomach, that he's sick & doesn't know what to do about it, goes back to the toilet, throws up some more, comes back out, gives me a paperbag he says he wants me to keep for him until he comes for it. I hide the bag under some shirts & underwear in a drawer. He takes off down the street, huddled up, looks like he's going to be sick again, out in the cold, under the naked trees. Will I ever see him again???

What will they mean, these nervous notes 10 yrs from today, 15, 20, 30 yrs.—will I live to see 30 yrs. from today?

March ??

Flunked chem exam. Mr. Schulman says, "MC, I really was expecting a lot more from you" but got 3 new tunes wrote last night, good ones I'm not even sure our band can play.

Must learn more abt theory, etc., don't dig my arrangements that much anymore.

Rosie Salah writes tunes too & did one she thought we would like called *Rose of Tangiers,* has nice Afro-Latin tinge but too jazzy for us Mr. Salah thinks.

Going to start sitting in w/ jazz players every chance I get.

Donna Lee tells me her father has a lot of bks on jazz & on Langston Hughes that I could use for the paper I'm writing for Engl. Comp. Heavy little chick.

March 15

One of those beautiful summer-like Saturdays at the end of winter where you float thru the sexy streets & everything smells green & new & like the earth even if it's only in your head.

You meet somebody on the steps of the public library, it's a girl, she's attractive, the meeting has been prearranged, she's wearing tennis shoes, jeans, black sweater & a blue silk scarf around her neck, it's Donna Lee. You sit on the steps, talking, shy, & discuss the papers you have to do & both of you admit that you haven't even begun them yet & they're due in 2 weeks. She confesses that she has always wanted to talk w/ you alone & not just in the hall between classes but you always seemed so preoccupied w/ other things, your music? what? You tell her about your paper & she tells you about hers again & then the talk runs out & you just nod to everything she says & sit grinning like a cretin. You end up walking her all the way from the library on Woodward & Kirby to her house on Owens St., the east side. It's dusk & some people are just coming out of the Champion Bar to get some eats & some other people are just going in. She says Daddy doesn't like for her & her sisters to be around there after it gets dark out, too many drunks & crazy people. You can smell suppers cooking all up & down her block, roasts, hams, chickens, chops, beans, greens, cornbreads, pies.

You try & say goodbye at the door but she insists that you come in & meet her Dad & get those bks, so in you go, get introduced to her 2 younger sisters, Mama's in the kitchen measuring rice into a cup, Daddy's having himself a beer & engrossed in the news on television, says he's heard a lot about you & enjoyed that record you made, not bad, not bad, have a seat, smoke?, he smoked when he was your age he says but he didn't let on that he did, stay for dinner, O you must, I know you must like pot roast, how far do you live from here?, what are your plans in this music racket?, sure you wouldn't like a cigarette? Her father is an interesting man, a machinist at Ford's, worked his way thru a year of college at the end of the Depression before the War broke out, there was a fellow who tried to teach him guitar in the service but he never got any further than the chords C, F, & G7.

You like them very much, good food, a real family that seems to have fun & get along w/ one another.

You know you'll be back.

THREE

I DID get to know Donna Lee and her family a lot better. I wasnt able to visit them as often as I would have liked that spring because it came to the point where I would have to do or die insofar as my studies were concerned, if you could call them studies. Shakes, Jimmy and I were all in the same boat. It was sink or swim. Both Claude and Mr. Salah were leaning on me. Mr. Salah literally wanted to get the show on the road.

It would be necessary, first of all, to get all the late-night fooling around put aside, as much as I enjoyed it. No-Doz was no longer doing the trick in keeping me awake and I had begun to fool around with Dexamil, reducing spansules, that Shakes had been using with some success. However, they threw my whole system off and it would take me days to recover.

For Shakes, to hear him talk, school wasnt that much of a problem. "I aint learnin a damn thing, MC, but at least I can leaf thru that jive and look at it kinda hard and come back up with about seventy-five percent when it's time to regurgitate. Take that last test in Spanish we had. Miss Van Camp hit us with all that heavy vocabulary and I threw it right back at her. Now, far as talkin and rappin in Spanish is concerned, I cant hardly even say 'how do you do' but I can jive. Jivin is what's happenin! Same in chem. That's some cold-blooded shit they put on us in there but I can flat get down with they ass and be just as cold-blooded. That's how them paddy kids be doin it. I was checkin out Paul Gross and Ronnie McLaughlin on that last test, lookin dead at em, and they had equations and formulas wrote all over they fingernails and cross they watchbands and all down between they toes for all I knew, and even had a set of signals worked up to trade answers. All Schulman had to do was take one walk down the aisle to the back of the room and both of em wouldve been expelled. But now, you watch! Theyll probably end up makin the honor roll just behind such jive as that. Learn to jive, baby, that's what everybody else is doin!"

"I know, man, but all I wanna do is get outta this place, and get on to whatever the next thing is."

"I know what you mean."

"How you feel about this thing we're into now, man? Are you diggin it, this playin and stuff?"

"I intend to get all I can out the deal, baby. But I dont know if I trust Abdullah all that much. I think he usin us."

"Maybe so, but we're usin him too. That's how it works. People use one another. We let ourselves be used till we can get in a position where we can ask a little higher price."

"Dont you think I know that? I done figured it out too, you know—and it's a lotta things I want before I get outta this world, jack, and I been wantin em a long time. My old man been wantin em, my old lady been wantin em. You oughtta see how nice my old man been now that I'm startin to knock down a few coins. Remember how the cat use to all the time be up in my face and standin on my head? Now he be talkin bout, 'Well, it looks as if you finally might make something out of yourself, James'—puttin his big, serious voice on me, dig it. 'I dont know how far your drumming's going to carry you but maybe one day youll be able to pay us back some of what we paid for them.' He still pushin for me to go to college tho and maybe get into social work or somethin. But I dont pay the cat no mind. I might end up supportin him one of these days."

"What about your mother?"

"Aw, I dont wanna even go into that. She says she's scared for me, hopes I dont get into any trouble. That chick is pretty sharp tho, my old lady. She can tell when I'm kinda half messed-up even if I only had a coupla swigs of brew. I have to put up a helluva show round her, and I dont know how much longer I can keep that shit up."

"Same with Claude. She says she's scared for me, too. She's really scared I'm gonna cut out."

"Cut out for where?"

"Anywhere, wherever the gig takes us. Detroit isnt the world, you know."

He paused and toyed with his newly sprouted chin whiskers. "Yeah, I been tryna figger my scene out too, what I'mo do when school is out. In a way, you luckier than I am, man."

"In what sense?"

"You only got a grandmother to fight. I got two folks to fight and they some stubborn people too. My old man been sellin that insurance too long. He dont think it's nothin to life but havin a good job, a choice slave, you dig, and meetin them notes and keepin up a front. He aint as bad as some of these e-lites but the cat shakes me up sometime."

"Well, I'd just like to learn more about life, get out and do a little travelin around."

"You gon learn about that no matter what you do, the way I see it. See, you really are different from me, man. You actually *like* readin books and takin stuff seriously, philosophizin and shit. Me. I just wanna get down all the hip licks so I can get with the people that's playin the hip licks and pull me down some bread. You watch, I'mo get me a sportcar yet. Get me a sportcar and some clothes and start stalkin bitches, man! Both our times is comin. You wait and see."

"Billy Sanchez wants to study music formally but I think he's gonna make his mark in jazz."

"He gon make it too, that little blind nigger can cook his butt off! Sometime he make me wish I was in his shoes and couldnt see nothin. Cat's got an ear and a half when it comes to all that way-out modern stuff."

"One dude I cant seem to figger out tho is Jimmy Monday. He never says much of anything at all, he's so cool, super-cool."

"That's the secret, stay cool, be cool. Jimmy know where it's at. But he scares me when he start talkin bout joinin the Navy."

"Me, too—where's he get that from?"

"From his brother, I think, his brother was in the Navy and never got over it. Funny stud but I can dig him."

"We're all funny."

"Yes, I know, MC. Tell me somethin else that's profound."

"Listen, I'd like to see us do more jazz things. We could really stretch out if we wanted to. Why couldn't we really work out a nice little mixture of blues and jazz. I think thatd sell."

"Maybe so, but the jazz dudes we been runnin

into lately dont seem to be workin all that much with that weird space shit they be puttin down. What you dont seem to understand, MC, is we got a groovy little thing goin on right now. That's the trouble with you, man, you never satisfied with where you at, you always got to be movin on to somethin else."

"Cant help it."

"I think we both need to get away from this old school grind for awhile. Why dont we go out and fuck up tonight? It's Friday, man. I dont know bout you but I been crammin shit in my head for four days in a row and now I cant even hardly see straight no more. Let's go out and party!"

"Nah, not me. I dont have a photographic memory like you do. About the only way I know to master this shit is to haul ass and study."

"Aw, Negro, that's all you ever do is work! If you aint studyin you practicin or readin or worryin your grandmama. She got to realize that you got your life to lead too."

"Tell your folks that."

"All right, OK, man–like, truce, OK? Look, I know where it's a party tonight–Erica Dobson, that e-lite broad that live on Boston Boulevard is givin one. We could break by there."

"I cant stand those people, man, those jive-ass, phony e-lites, they get on my nerves."

"Why dont you fall back to the pad and think about it? I'll go back to my place, get togged down, hit a joint or two, and come by for you round nine. I aint crazy bout them people neither but I dont let that prejudice my view of partyin.

Fuck em, we'll come anyway, drink they liquor, eat they food and dance with they broads. I happen to know Wimp and them they gon be on the set. He blowin trumpet with Andy Coleman's group and they got the gig to play the party, so we can even bring our axes and sit in." Shakes snickered. "Or maybe you would rather sit home and write shit in your diary about how tough Donna Lee Jackson is!"

In a good mood I had made the mistake of showing him some pages from my journal. Never again!

I had been pushing myself severely lately and his idea did have some appeal since it meant an opportunity to sit in with Andy Coleman's band. They played OK dance jazz but nothing special, and they had never shown any envy toward us like a lot of the other bands around had after our record came out.

"I'll be by in my old man's short to pick you up round nine—and this time be ready for a change!"

FOUR

I LUGGED my guitar and amp to the party but Shakes only had to bring a pair of sticks since the band's regular drummer would already be set up. "Sometimes I envy Billy," I told him. "He never has to worry about draggin a piano around."

"Maybe not, but he sure gets to play on some bogue, bad-soundin boxes, poor cat. I dont envy nobody."

"I'm glad we can play, man, otherwise we might have to talk to those people and you know what a drag that could be."

"You see me doin up this pot, dont you? I aint about to waste my good high rappin with them stuck-up cute niggers. Sure you dont want some of this?"

"You know I cant play behind that stuff."

"Well, I sure the hell can. Mmmm, and this some good shit too. This some stuff Champ laid on me back last summer that I'd done hid in my basement back of the furnace and forgot about. What's that joker up to these days anyway?"

"Search me. He fell by sick a few weeks back. Good thing Claude wasnt around, she mightve called the police. Cat looked bad, man. I mean bad-bad, he was so messed up he couldnt hardly walk. He was throwin-up sick. Made me nervous."

"Sound like he might be into some heavy shit. I asked one of the chicks round on Euclid bout him the other night and she said he hadnt been comin around but that some people'd come by lookin for him, some rough-lookin people. Cat better watch his step. I think he probably strung out."

"Come to think of it, he left a bag when he was by, a paperbag he said he wanted me to hold for him."

"Get rid of it, get rid of it. The Masters of Ceremony cannot afford to be gettin into any bad hassles, especially with drugs," Shakes advised, steering the car around the corner onto Boston Blvd. with one hand and butting the joint in the ashtray with the other. He dropped the butt, the roach, down his throat, swallowed it, and grunted, "Like the man say, you got to get rid of that evidence."

Parties were something I wasnt used to and as soon as we hit the door I sensed it was going to be a real ordeal. Shakes, contrary to what he'd said on the way over, was loaded and eager to mix with everybody. "A well-appointed pad, MC, if I must say so myself—fabulous, fabulous indeed! Let's get our heads bad and get down with these mucky-mucks."

No one seemed to mind that we were there though uninvited. Erica herself was rather proud, in fact, that we had turned up, and at once began trotting us around to show off. She must take us for a couple of poodles, I thought, but went along with the program anyway. Her folks were away for the weekend, so there was no parental supervision, and plenty to eat and drink.

I started in on beer but later switched to Scotch which I chased down with ginger ale, so you can imagine about how long I was going to last. All the guys in the band were juicing it up. Andy Coleman himself was in a good mood, running all his Sonny Rollins and Coltrane licks down on tenor sax and sounding very, very professional. He was an older musician, older by our standards, who kept a loosely knit unit together for working house parties and weekend dances. Detroit was full of musicians. Andy was an old friend of Champ's and at one time I had admired the glib, solid effect he got on his horn, but that was before I'd really gotten to know who was who and what was what. He was proficient in bringing off musically the kind of thing that Shakes did with textbooks. Still, the band sounded good and when Andy recognized us he asked if we would like to sit in.

"Thatd be a groove, man," I said, feeling mellow at the moment.

"Wait till next set, we should be warmed up by then."

We stood around warming ourselves up. Kids in nice clothes and a little drunk kept coming over to say something. They werent as snotty as I had expected. One chick even asked me to dance. I didnt dance well but accepted anyway, feeling clumsy and self-conscious in my plain suit and tie. I hated suits and ties. Most of these kids' parents were doctors, lawyers, social-climbing administrators and schoolteachers—definitely out of my class. Even though many of us attended the same public school and knew one another by name, I understood that they looked down on people like Shakes and myself and never asked us to their sniffy gatherings. Erica's old man ran a big funeral parlor in a poor black section on the east side and his picture was always in the colored papers, the society section, sometimes even in the white papers. He had been written up many times in *Ebony* magazine.

Everyone smelled so nice and looked so smug.

Erica herself, whom I had always thought to be pretty saditty and stuck on herself, was actually one of the warmest and most charming girls there. "MC, would you like something to eat? Youre always so shy and lonesome-looking. This is a party, for crying out loud—enjoy yourself, things cant be that bad."

I wondered what Erica and the others hoped to make of their lives. What did girls like her have to look forward to besides a university degree, an expensive house or apartment in a section of town away from the riffraff, i.e., people like me and the neighborhood I lived in? Of course, theyd want a super-educated man with a responsible job who was shaking down a princely salary and steady building up prestige on the side. I imagined that they wanted a new car every year and a half, sportscars, fine clothes, jet flight vacations, several color TV sets, twin ovens, twin refrigerators, twin washers, twin dryers, sunken bathtubs, color phones, stereo, luxurious carpets, imported liquor, art seminars in the home, Steinway pianos, delicate china, flashing silver, pool tables, pools, tennis courts; genteel gatherings on Sunday afternoons on lush evenly trimmed green green lawns surrounded by hedges, the swish of silk and tinkle of ice-cubes absorbed up into the crisp accredited air. Did they aspire to anything besides the neuroses of half-hip white people who imitate Europeans imitating Americans?

"O, I dont know about Stanley," I overheard one girl saying to another, "I think he's going thru some kind of identity crisis just now."

Maybe what made Erica seem so relaxed compared to the general run of those girls there that night was that she knew her folks were on top of it all, if you subscribed to that game of I-can-afford-to-get-more-into-debt-than-you-can-&-still-be-respectable-too. If you could keep up with the Dobsons, you didn't have to worry about those trashy Joneses.

These people were Americans, and Americans were something I still had to learn about. "Wouldnt that be a gas," I told Shakes when I found him, "to be an American, wouldnt that be weird?"

"I dont know about you but I was brought up on grits and Kool-Aid."

By the time it came time for us to sit in, I was more than a little tipsy. I was half tore-up but determined to play. Shakes floated up to the stand and came down behind the drums. I warmed my fingers up on the fretboard and waited for Andy to call a tempo.

He called a current tune in a tempo I really wasnt ready for but I tried to lay with it anyway by halving the time meter of my solo and gliding. I knew the bass player's hands were about to fall off because mine were. Shakes held up like a little champion. When the tune was over I noticed that people had stopped dancing and were standing around listening. Wimp macked over with his trumpet tucked under his arm like some dixieland cowboy and whispered to me loud enough for Shakes to hear: "You niggers been smokin some powerful shit—turn me on!"

That made me mad.

Andy called a ballad next but after the first chorus upped the tempo to a bright, medium groove, and then, during my solo, kept messing around with the key, changing it on the bridge, changing it back again at the coda, anything to keep me on edge.

I was feeling sick to my stomach and wanted to get up and leave the stand. When I picked up my foot to move the amp back, my whole leg began to tremble. "Somethin the matter, man?" Shakes called out from above.

"I dont know. I dont feel good. I'll be right back."

There was some applause as I stepped off the stand but I knew that no one could really be serious. When I looked back, I saw Wimp shaking his head dolefully in my direction.

In the bathroom, trying to get straight, I realized just how drunk I was. I dabbed sweat from my cheeks and forehead with a tissue, combed my hair, adjusted my clothes, spotted a paperback on a table next to the toilet and sat down on the upholstered stool to leaf thru it. I couldnt even bring the words into focus. Somebody was knocking at the door, a girl's voice saying, "Please can I come in, I'll only be a minute."

"Come on in, I cant move!"

It was Joyce, the girl I'd been dancing with earlier. Her eyes popped when she saw me but she was cool. She broke out laughing. "Really, MC, is this any place to be catching up on your reading? Is it good?"

I didn't want to say anything because then she would know I was out of my mind, so I started laughing too. I must have looked ridiculous, now that I thought of it. "I suppose you could make yourself at home in a place like this." The bathroom, which was the size of an average livingroom, did have bookshelves, a magazine rack, FM radio, wall-to-wall carpeting, the works.

I rose and weaved toward the door. Joyce caught my arm as I passed by. "Are you all right, are you ill? If you need a ride home, Ive got a car and there's plenty of room in back for your equipment."

"No, no, I'm OK, go ahead . . ."

"All right, if you say so, but if you feel like you might want to go home, remember I offered. I'll be right out if youll just wait outside the door."

"Sure." I got ahold of Shakes and asked him to look after my gear and see that it got packed.

Outside in the backyard where I stumbled for some fresh air, couples were mulling, whispering in the dark.

No stars were up.

In the distance I could hear the band pumping thru some old *Heart and Soul* changes, Shakes' discreet sock cymbal accents swishing off and on in just the right places. For a moment they sounded like the backup band in the pit of the old Empress Burlesk at the foot of Woodward.

Everybody's got their damn band, I was thinking. Who said that? We've got our band, the e-lites got their band, the eastside, the westside, the rich and the raggedy, the listeners, the dancers, the Army, the Navy, Roy Rogers and Hitler.

FIVE

WITHOUT SO MUCH as looking back, I walked all the way from Boston Blvd. over to the John Lodge Expressway cross Woodward down Clairmount past Northern High School. At first I wobbled but the long walk and the air and the fact that it wasnt a warm night and I had on nothing but a suit jacket must have helped sober me. I still felt drunk but wasnt worried about it. Just a loon clicking down the street with his hands in his pockets, whistling bullshit.

Some young teenagers were standing on a corner singing one of the last of the doo-wah tunes. I stopped to listen and could tell that one of the guys was really good. He could cut a record too if some promoter could just get to him and give him a break. Maybe one day some slick joker would hit town and wise up to how much music went on around here, good music, and start a record company and record everybody and make a fortune.

I took up the kids' tune myself and did all the parts, all the way to Owens St., Donna Lee's block.

leaving the whole
cozy kitchen
quiet

SIX

THE DEVIL is beating his wife!

It's raining in late spring and the sun is shining anyway.

Claude always said, when she saw that happening, that the devil was beating his wife.

I would rather describe this light, this beautiful light, that pours thru the window and onto my arms and chest and the paper I write on than lay down words to describe the sadness I felt that June when nothing seemed to be working out as planned.

I graduated from school all right, all of us did. I barely got out by the skin of my teeth. Mr. Schulman passed me in chem out of sheer mercifulness. "Youre no scientist, MC, but I'm expecting you to make a name for yourself one of these days."

The studyhall counselor, Mr. Jacobs, had said something similar. "It isnt every day that we have the opportunity of graduating someone who's already gotten their career underway. Best of luck on your musical career, MC. I'm sorry to say that I havent had the pleasure of hearing your group play or your recording but my daughter assures me that you have a lot of talent. Youre a credit to your race." Or something like that.

Claude cried at the graduation ceremony that morning, the first time I had known her to do so in public. Seeing her, I felt as if I ought to be shedding a tear too but couldnt quite work myself up to it. "You made it, MC, you made it, darlin! Now youre a high school graduate! O, I'm so proud of you! Come here and let me hug you!"

Jezzy had come along to keep Claude company. "Congratulations, MC. I'm glad you made it. I feel like it's one of my boys that's gettin out and all three of them done graduated and left home a long time ago. Here's a little present for you. Dont open it till you get home."

Shakes' folks were there. I wondered if his mother still planned to ring up the draft board and have them send him one of their infamous greetings. I could tell by the look on their faces that they felt more relieved than anything else.

That night at the dance, while everybody else was busy sneaking out in the parkinglot to get a taste or hit a couple of tokes, I danced every dance but three with Donna Lee and, cold sober, told her that I dug her. The word *love* was OK to put in a diary but seemed a little serious face-to-face.

Some old corny number they had us waltzing to almost sounded like the real thing.

"What are your plans," she asked, "now that youre out of Sing Sing?"

"Out of Sing Sing is right. I dont know, I'd like to travel maybe."

"The other night you told me you might go to college."

"I dont know if any college would let me in with my grades."

"You have to apply first, you know."

"Yeah, I know. I'll probably go—eventually. For now, I gotta figger out what the band's gonna do. We're supposed to travel around and work some jobs this summer."

"I wouldnt want you to go away, MC, not for very long anyway, not too far away either."

That night when I got her home and was again making that senseless tender small-talk on her porch that two people make when they really have no intention of saying goodnight, Mr. Jackson came to the door and frightened us both by clearing his throat, barely visible in his robe and pajamas behind the screendoor. "O, hi, Daddy!"

"Good morning, young lady. Good morning, young man."

"I was just telling Donna goodnight, Mr. Jackson, we really had a nice time at the dance."

"I'm glad to see you had a nice time, MC, but do you know that it's getting on towards four o'clock *tomorrow?* I go for a nice time too but it's time now for people to be in off the streets, people that have homes."

"Yessir, I was just going myself."

"Do you need busfare? I'd be glad to lend it to you, or dont the buses still run this time of night?"

"Yes, theyre runnin. I was just gonna say goodnight."

"I think Ive already heard you say goodnight—about sixteen times to be exact. Donna Lee, you know I'm happy for both of you and I realize it's a big occasion, but will you kindly come in the house and go to bed. Your mother and I have been worried to death about you. I had to make her take a sleepingpill and put her to bed."

I started down the steps. Mr. Jackson called after me. "MC!"

"Yessir."

"Would you come back up here a minute."

"Yessir."

"Since you were the one made me smoke up all my cigarettes pacing the floor, not knowing whether or not you were ever gonna bring my oldest daughter back—"

"I'm sorry, Mr. Jackson, but we got hung up."

"Now, you wouldnt try to lay a hype on an old hepcat like me, would you? I was saying—since you made me smoke up all my cigarettes, I think it's only fair that you let me bum a couple of yours."

"I hope you dont mind Kools."

"I'm not prejudiced. In fact, some of my best friends are penguins."

SEVEN

FROM NOT working together enough since winter, and because our ideas about things were changing so quickly now that we were all out of school with nothing to hold us back, the band had fallen into very bad shape.

While the rest of us had been busy hacking those books, Billy Sanchez had lost interest in playfor the group and was working around town fulltime with some of the jazz groups. That had always been his thing anyway. One of his heroes was Yusef Lateef, the great reed player, and Billy had always spoken of going to New York to be near him. He was always figuring out methods of improving himself. A few days after graduation, he was asked by the leader of a prominent group out of New York to join them for the rest of the summer at least. The band, with the blessings of Billy's folks, took our boy away from us, claiming it was only for an eight-week tour. "Listen, I'll put in a word for yall everyplace I go," Billy told me, but something else told me that he was leaving Detroit for good. One of our strongest members, stolen right out from under us! We'd never be able to replace him.

Billy's leaving upset Jimmy Monday and he

started talking that Navy talk of his more seriously than ever.

Morale went down all around.

Snakes had been completely forgotten. Abdullah Salah informed me that since we had already fulfilled our legal obligations he wasnt too anxious to sign us again. He suggested that we organize ourselves along new lines, work up an act, get a style down, and get to work rehearsing new material, professional arrangements that Moonbeam would pay for if we were willing to co-operate. I asked him what he had in mind.

"I dont think you guys really want to go professional yet. You took your own sweet time about keeping appointments with me all during the spring. I understand that you were trying to get out of school and all, but youve got to realize, MC, that this is a business like any other business. I could have gotten you bookings for this summer but you guys didnt seem to know what you wanted to do. Now one of your best men's left the band. There's a whole new trend moving in now and the sort of thing you had going with *Snakes* is pretty old hat by now. Things move fast, youve got to keep up. You dont know whether you want to play jazz or blues or make a living or anything."

"What about if we just keep on playin good music."

"MC, MC, listen to me. Work up a new act and a new book and I can book you out with some of these packages that work places like the Greystone. You wouldnt make that much at first and your name might not be at the top of the bill but with proper management you could work yourselves up into real headliners. I still have a lot of faith in you fellows. And just between you and me, this rhythm and blues and soul music is going to skyrocket into one helluva business. Believe me, I can feel when something is right, when the time is right. But, if you want to stay on with Moonbeam and have me for a manager, youre going to have to talk to the boys in your band and get them to make up their minds damn quick about your plans. Ive got a couple of other bands that are champing at the bit for a start. They may not be as good as your group musically, but theyve got real potential as showmen, performers, and that's what I'd like for you fellows to work on. Think it over. Talk it over."

I thought it over and talked it over with Shakes and Jimmy. Shakes' parents were pulling to get him away from music. His father had walked in on him smoking pot down in the basement and had slapped him around quite brutally. Some of the bruises still showed.

"Bogue nigger, must dont know who he messin with," Shakes complained to me. "Flushed all my good boo down the toilet too and talkin bout callin the law on me, his own son. Can you get to that, MC? His own flesh and blood! First, I was gon get me a gun and shoot the nigger but somethin told me that was the wrong thing to do. I'mo leave home, that's what I'mo do. Wait and see. I'mo figger me out a way to get my drums packed and shipped someplace, get all my rags together and split, cut both of em loose. Big a juicehead as he is, he gon fuck me round over some gauge. Shit, you know it's gon be hard for me and him to even live under the same roof from here on out."

"Did your mother do anything?"

Shakes looked away from me and rubbed at that scraggly red goatee of his. "She was depressin. She just cried, man, just cried, cried for days. That was almost harder to take than my old man's planned and deliberate assault on me. Joker sprained my wrist too when he slapped me off that stool. I aint been able to do a press roll worth a damn since."

"Itll heal, man. Youll forget about the whole thing."

"The hell I will. I'm makin plans to swoop." He went on to explain how his folks thought that music was a bad influence on him, and that most musicians were essentially degenerate, unless they played accepted, official, inoffensive music, of course. "And they think you stone crazy, MC."

"Me?"

"Yeah, you. You oughtta heard my old lady talkin about how you look like you dont get regular meals and how your mind always seems to be someplace else. 'That boy gon drive himself crazy if he's not careful!' They talkin bout sendin me someplace to learn a trade. I told em I already got a trade, I'm a percussionist. You watch, man, they say they gon cut me off if I leave home but I'mo have to do it, or my name aint James Shakespeare Harris, Jr.—forget the Jr.!"

Jimmy Monday who was silent, except when the conversation directly concerned either bass playing or automobiles, told me that we should have gotten a better understanding with Abdullah Salah from the onset. "I'm signing up with the Navy, MC. I can either go into the band there and travel around, or get into something like metallurgy which has always interested me. My brother says it isnt such a bad deal, especially now that theyre opening up more doors for the black man."

"You really think that's where it's at, Jimmy? Youre a good musician, you know, and if we stick it out maybe we might be able to do something for ourselves."

"You know me. I enjoy playing as much as the next guy, but I'm not really that big on gigs or on making a living off music. It's nice for a little pocket money now and then but after a while it's no fun. I like it when we work out at rehearsals or just to be getting together. I even enjoyed some of the jobs we got off of that record, but let's look at the facts—our record sold pretty well around here for a while and we made a few hundred dollars apiece off of it. Now it's all played out and Abdullah doesnt want to release our other record, you say, because he wants us to set out in another direction, to keep up with the times, right? I say the hell with him. The hell with him and the whole crummy music business! Ive watched my Uncle Joe over the years. He knows how to do it. He works for Moonbeam but that's just one of the things he's doing. He drives that big truck of his around hauling a couple of days a week and pretty soon he'll be finally opening that barbecue place and getting out of the music business which he never was sold on anyway. I dont feel like I'm sold on it either, man. I go with the Navy and I know that that three square is gonna be there on the table, seven days a week. I can find a band to play with in there the same as Ive always found a band to play with since the eighth grade at Hutchins. I dig playing in bands, and I dig fixing cars but I enjoy both things so much that I'm not so sure I'd care to make a living at either one. That's why I'm going to look into this metallurgy thing. Now, there's a real possibility too, a chance to pick up on a trade and not really feel that I'm compromising myself."

Who would ever have thought that that long tall Jimmy Monday with his thick hair parted on one side and who turned up at sessions in his greasy coveralls, puffing on a pipe full of Balkan Sobranie, would come up with a statement like that when it finally came down to the nitty-gritty?

Every Man for Himself was the name of the game.

EIGHT

CHAMP SENT for me.

Unfortunately, Claude got to the phone first when the call came in. "It's for you, MC."

"Who is it, Mr. Salah?"

"Naw, it's a woman's voice but it dont sound to me like Donna Lee."

"Hello."

"Hello, MC? Listen, baby, this is Claire."

"Who?"

"Claire, remember? You met me thru Champ."

My heart started thumping and I tensed up. Claude pretended to not be listening as she carefully put her numbers gear away. She would have to be leaving to catch her bus in a minute. Jezzy had just left. It was almost seven-thirty.

"Yes, yes, well, what is it, Mrs. Cole?" I said into the receiver. Cole was Champ's last name. "What can I do for you?"

"Hunh? What old goddamn Mrs. Cole? This aint no Mrs. Cole, this is Claire. Now, I know you havent forgotten about me that quick, baby. That night, your first time, remember? I notice you havent bothered to come back, what's the matter, you scared of me?"

"No, Mrs. Cole."

Claude was frozen in her place at the drawer and looking dead at me. I was only hoping she wouldnt be able to hear the other end of the conversation.

"I dont know what kinda bullshit game you tryna run on me, MC, but your friend Champ the one asked me to call you."

"Champ? Is there somethin the matter, Mrs. Cole?"

"You better believe it's somethin the matter, Mr. MC. Somebody done tried they best to kill his ass and he layin up here hurt say he want you to come see him."

"He's at hime now, hunh?"

"O, I get it—damn! I near bout forgot, you still living at home, aint you? Was that your mama answered? I get it. Excuse me, baby, but listen—Champ got in some trouble with some men and got done in pretty bad, and—"

"Is he all right?"

"He aint in too good a shape but he can talk, he can even move a little bit but not that much."

"O no, I'm really sorry to hear that, Mrs. Cole! Is there anything I can do?"

"Heh, yeah, you sure can, you can get your butt over here and talk with him. He keeps askin for you, keeps sayin, 'MC, MC, I wanna see MC.' So I told him I'd call you."

"What would be a good time for me to come see him, Mrs. Cole?"

"Your mama gon get suspicious sure enough you keep saying Mrs. Cole over and over like that. Come as soon as you can, up here to the place. You know where I stay."

"OK, I'll be by. I hope he gets better. I know how bad you must feel about it, Mrs.—yeah, OK, I'll be there as soon as I can take care of a few things and catch a bus."

"And one more thing, MC."

"Yes, yes."

"Champ say to bring the bag."

"Yes, ma'am, I'll be glad to stop off and pick you up somethin on the way over. What is it you need?"

"The bag, MC. Champ say he gave you a bag to hold for him. Bring it when you come."

"Some aspirin, all right, I'll pick some up at Thad's on my way over. Goodbye."

Claude looked at me for a long time after I hung up. I knew she was waiting to hear what I would say before she made any remark. How well you get to know a person after years together in the same house. "That was Mrs. Cole, Claude, Champ's mother. He's hurt."

"What happen to him?"

"He got in an accident of some kind and he's laid up in bad shape."

"Hmmph! That's too bad. Hurt in an accident, hunh? What was it, a car accident or what?"

"She didnt say. She isnt sure. Some people brought him home and he hasnt fully recovered his senses yet."

"Why didnt they take him to a hospital?"

"Dont ask me, Claude, I'm just telling you what she told me."

She went into her purse and handed me a ten-dollar bill. "Here, this is for them groceries I want you to pick up at the A&P for me. I cant miss my bus, MC. I use to could tell when you was lyin, right off—but lately it's been so much jive and mess goin on round here till I dont hardly know what to make of anything anymore. But I'll tell you one thing—I'mo have that durn phone number changed and a new lock put on the door and start back to readin the Bible more. That's what I'm do! I dont know what you been doin but what goes around comes around. Tell Champ's mama I'm sorry to hear bout his accident. I never was crazy bout the child but I know she must be goin thru some misery if it's really anything like you tell me it is. See you later, baby. Now dont you go out and get in an accident too, hear?"

"Claude?"

"Champ's mama sure has a sweet young voice, sound like she cant be much older than you," she called back on her way out. "Be careful!"

I never thought I could fool her completely. I only wanted to smooth over an embarrassing situation and get the thing over with.

I was becoming a little afraid—for Champ, for myself, for Claude, for Shakes, for all of us.

NINE

THEY HAD Champ propped up on a pillow in bed. The pillowcase and sheet seemed freshly starched and ironed but there was a dirty ball of bed linen in a corner nearby as well as trousers, shirt, jacket; all of it frighteningly bloodstained. Claire, Leona and Michele had been taking turns looking after him; washing his wounds, applying antiseptics and bandaging him.

"What happened, Claire? What happened exactly?"

"He rung the doorbell last night and when Michele went down to open the door he stumbled in and fell up against her and they both went down. I was up here sprayin the place down with Air-Wick and heard her scream. First I thought it was a raid but then Michele hollered, 'Come get him up offa me!' so then I didnt know what to think. I went and got my .38 out the shoebox in the clothes-closet and tipped out into the hall and peeped round the corner to see what the hell was comin down. I liked to died! Champ was layin all on toppa that poor little girl and'd done got blood all over that dress she'd just ironed. She say, 'It's Champ, Claire, it's Champ!' Talk about scared, I thought he was dead! I didnt know what to do. Leona was back in her room takin care of some business but Michele's hollerin musta shook them up too because they both came runnin out here half-naked and saw me standin on the landin over Champ and Michele with that gun in my hand, shakin like a leaf. The john say, 'What happen, you shoot somebody? Damn, lemme get my clothes on and get the fuck outta here! I come up here for a piece of tail and get mixed up in some old ignorant murder shit!' Michele hollerin, 'Please help me somebody, come get him up offa me, he's hurt and he's hurtin me!' So the man and Leona came down and the three of us pulled Champ up offa Michele and dragged him up the steps to my room. He looked pretty damn bad too—eyes all closed up, cuts all cross his face and blood all over him, but he was breathin and gruntin and kept sayin he was all right, for us to lay him down someplace. So we laid him down cross my bed but he kept on whining and carryin on like it was a bone broke. We didnt wanna call no doctor and I thought the man, Leona's trick, might know of somebody could help us. He said he'd done done his part and threw his clothes on and shot outta here."

"Well, did you get a doctor for him?"

"Yeah, finally. Geechy knew one, some chump we could count on to take care of Champ and not put our business in the street if the police came around. Geechy got his man up here and dressed Champ, gave him some shots and bandaged and stitched him up."

"No broken bones?"

"Naw, not that he could tell, but a lotta stitches, stitches all over his body. Nigger got five hundred dollars' worth of thread holdin him together."

"Who did it? Why?"

"You ask too many questions, baby. He say it look like to him it musta been two or three of em was after him and laid for him. But I dont know a bit more bout what Champ been doin than a man in the moon. He know who did it. He on some kinda sleepin pill now but he oughta be wakin up in a little while. Itll be time for his shot soon."

"O, did the doctor put him on some kind of antibiotic?"

"Antibiotic my ass! Champ is strung out, honey —cut up or not cut up he still got to have that hit twice a day."

"What's he shootin?"

"You bring that bag?"

"Here it is."

She unfolded it and looked down inside as I had done before leaving the house, so panicked about getting there as fast as I could that I hadnt bothered to inspect the bag's contents more closely. Claire poured out twenty or so glassine envelopes onto a dresser, and a small oblong newspaper-wrapped package. Inside the news wrap was a plastic bag and inside that a syringe.

Never having liked needles anyway, I came as close to fainting as it's possible to do without falling out.

She administered the shot while I looked the other way and then took off, leaving me alone with Champ in her room.

He looked like Frankenstein. He looked manufactured and unreal; something sewn together by a madman. His flesh had the texture of thick brown bumpy celluloid.

It was one of those muggy midwest afternoons and the drawn raggedy windowshade was soiled and yellow with hot sunlight trying to seep thru its creases and around the edges. I stared at the windowshade rather than at Champ. I felt sorry for him, laid up, sweating, stitches laced into him every whichway. Yet, now that he'd been shot up with his pitiful medicine, he blinked his eyes at me and tried to force a smile. "MC . . . hey . . . my man . . ."

"Hey, Champ. Look like you met with a bad accident, hunh?"

"Somethin like that."

"How do you feel?"

"Feel? Aint feelin too mucha nothin right now. What time is it, man? What day is it?"

"It's Tuesday, Tuesday around two in the afternoon."

"Mmmm . . ."

"You dont have to talk, you know. I just dropped in to see how you were."

"Doin? Yeah . . . I cant complain, man. Pretty fucked up but I cant complain . . . no. I'm hungry, man. They got anything to eat around this place?"

"They keep food here too?"

"Oughta be some type of pecks, somethin kinda light I can . . . grease on. I cant chew too good, man, so it's got to be soft, y'understand. They messed my teeth up, them motherfuckers, one of them kicked me in the mouth and fucked my teeth up. Them some cold motherfuckers, man, collllld . . . collllld! I feel cold too. You mind lettin the window down?"

As much as I hated to, I let the window down while he drifted away for a moment. He spotted the picture of the child in the frame on Claire's dresser. "Know who that is, MC? That's Claire's little boy. Chick got a kid somewhere, man." He turned his face back toward me and I noticed that a softness had come into his raw threaded face. "Look at me, MC, aint this some shit? I was tryna make it back to my pad after they tried to off me . . . but I just couldnt make it. This the closest place I could get to. They thought I was dead, man, they tried they best to annihilate my ass! No tellin how long I laid round there in that alley in the rain before I got the strength to move."

"Take it easy, man. I'll go see if they got anything to eat."

"Nice . . . niiiiiice . . ."

I found some Hershey bars and peanut butter in the pantry. It looked to me like ancient stuff. I sniffed and brought it to him anyway. He broke off one piece of chocolate and put it in his mouth. "I have to lay here and let it kinda melt, man . . . Cant move my jaws too much. Talk about jaws bein tight."

The time passed.

The whole place was more silent than I ever thought it got.

He'd doze off and drift back and talk out of his aching head. "I like you, MC. I go for you, man. Somethin bout you I always liked. You dont treat me like, like I'm shit—you know. Like all these other sick sonsabitches. You somethin like me, man. You dig what I dig, you dig them sounds. You know?"

I nodded.

"You still a young stud too, and you still got that certain thing."

"That certain thing?"

"Yeah. I dont know what you call it exactly . . . but it's that certain thing . . . and I feel for you, man, I really do."

Some more minutes slipped by but he came right back and picked up where he'd left off—

"What I mean by that certain thing is . . . like . . . it's like you be a certain way, when you aint crossed over that line yet."

"What line?"

"I call it . . . I call it that old fucked-up line, y'understand? You get what I'm gettin at?" He tried to move his arms and groaned. "Scuse me, man, but I'm itchin like a motherfucker! I'd scratch but that might . . . crack these damn strings that's keepin my ass together . . . mmmmm . . . What I mean . . . Whew! That was some down shit that broad fixed me with, I'mo *have* to scratch in a minute. Its like, it was a time back before I'd done crossed that old fucked-up line I'm talking bout—and I guess it's somethin like a bringdown, if you know what that is. Like, my old man, I aint laid eyes on that joker since I was five years old but from that time, say, up until I got to be round your age, fifteen, sixteen, seventeen, eighteen, someplace long in there, I still had that certain thing, that old young thing where everything still kinda funny, kinda strange, you know . . . and I wasnt too hip yet and didnt know what was happenin, can you dig it? Mmmm, you mind scratchin my back for me, man, but not too hard, just a little . . ."

As soon as I touched him, he twisted his head and told me to lighten up.

"Sorry, baby, but everything I do hurts. So then, after a certain amount of time'd done gone by, I'd done fucked up so bad, fucked around and fucked around and couldnt stay in school and got a police record—all that kinda shit. I got into all this stupid street shit and some more time pass and pretty soon I woke up one day and I didnt have that certain thing no more."

"Youre tryna say I'm still a kid, is that it?"

"Unh-unnnnh! Well, that too maybe but you got soul too, man, more than just a taste. You into this music thing heavy and you take it real serious which is nice, which is what I shoulda done, old fucked-up me. I stays kinda half high most of the time but it aint nothin else to do. If it was somethin better to do, I would get right up outta this godamn bed, stitches and all, and go out and do it. But now look at me—thought I was slick and slipped up, and dig!—"

"OK, OK. Take it easy, Champ."

"And people be thinkin I'm crazy and shit or aint got good sense and dont know what's happenin . . . but I be's steady diggin, diggin you and diggin everything else that be's goin down. So, when I tell you you got that certain thing, I mean you flat out got it. I would have it too myself—if I could play, if I could play like yall do. Hey, you bring any jams, man? You bring any Trane or Ornette or anything? You bring that jam yall made with you? What the hell's the name of it—*Shakes* or *Snakes* or whatever you call it?"

"You need to sleep, man, youre in bad shape."

"That's what I'm doin now. I'm sleep while I'm runnin this shit to you. This is a dream, MC. Relax, man. Aint nothin important. It's all bullshit . . . some bullshit! Do me this one favor. Call my old lady, baby. Call my old lady and tell her I'm hurt. Tell her I'm someplace hurt and cant get home."

"Should I tell her to come here where you are, or what?"

"Tell her—"

"Yeah?"

"Tell her . . . I'm hurt, man, like I'm hurt, hurt bad."

He dozed back off.

I waited for him to come around again but this time it looked as if he'd be sleeping for a while.

The last thing in the world I wanted to do was to have to be the one to call Champ's mother. I sat around watching him, waiting, stalling. I flipped thru a small pile of *Jet* magazines, hoping one of the girls would show up soon.

Finally, a little desperate, I rung up Shakes and told him what had happened, suggesting that, since he lived near Champ, perhaps he wouldnt mind going by and breaking the news to Mrs. Cole. He felt bad about the whole thing but explained that he didnt really want to get mixed up in the mess. He was growing more depressed by the day over his own predicament.

So I gave up and telephoned the poor woman. She sounded as though she had been weeping for days. Champ hadnt been home in a week. She thought he was dead but was afraid to bring the police into it because there was no telling what they might come up with. I tried to dress the story of her son's "accident" up, and at the same time tone it down.

The news broke her heart but she seemed glad to know he was still alive. She was going to call her brother out on his job and the two of them would be coming for Champ just as soon as they could.

I hung up relieved.

Had it been me on that bed, no matter what I'd done, I know I would have wanted Claude to know where I was.

TEN

4th July, 1:30 a.m.

Independence Day.

How nice it would be to be independent, truly independent. I don't know how much longer I can take this stage, if it's really just a stage. Something seems to have died in me. What is it? Why does all the bad luck come my way? Everything has changed. Shakes talks abt going to NYC but will not get up off of his behind & make the move, like Billy did. If he went I know I would go w/ him just to see what it's like there. Jimmy at least went down & enlisted yesterday. Good bass player gone berserk.

Champ is healing, on the outside at least, but his mother says that she is going to have to have him put into a hospital or clinic somewhere because she cannot afford to help him support his bad habits. I hope he doesn't end up in Lexington.

All the plans I had for the band are flying out the window. I can't seem to get along w/ Mr. Salah.

Sweet Donna Lee is my one bright spot in these dark moments. She got a job working in a bakery downtown for the summer. Last night I took the bus down to meet her when she got off work & she looked so worn-out in her uniform w/ flour all over it that eventually got on my coat. I asked what they had her doing all day & she said that she didn't know. Mr. Jackson has kindly invited me to spend the holiday w/ them & their family but I want to be w/ Claude. She's met a fellow at work that she talks abt & says is very intelligent. We're all supposed to spend the 4th w/ Jezzy & some of her friends & family at a big Bar-B. Q. on Belle Isle.

In the 7th grade when we were studying LaSalle, Chief Pontiac, Father Richard, Hazel Pingree & all of that Detroit history, one day Miss Luster told us about Belle Isle & how at one time it had been infested w/ snakes & how the French brought in pigs to get rid of them. The pigs got rid of the snakes all right but then they began to take over the island & ran wild. Shakes, who sat behind me in that class, leaned over & made a wisecrack under his breath that I will never forget. "So then they brought in the Negroes to barbecue the hogs & that's what they've been doing out there ever since."

It's been a long time since I've been on a picnic. Bo liked to take us on picnics, Big Bo who worked in a brickyard & told me to learn all I could abt "The Man" & how his systems work so that I would have what he called "a chance." When the weather was warm the 3 of us were always packing up huge pots of potato salad, sauce, slabs of ribs, baskets of paper plates, plastic spoons & napkins & heading for Belle Isle, Palmer Park or even to the country where Bo had friends who still lived the way I remember people living in the South. I loved it when the men played baseball with the children & there would be plenty of food to eat & lots of sodapop & firecrackers. I felt really at home then.

"Claude."

"Yes, MC."

"Can I talk to you?"

"Is it important, cause in a minute we gotta get all this mess packed up and in the car. I dont know bout you but I'm bout picnicked out! I wanna talk to you too when we get back home bout all that beer you drunk. I didnt know you could put away that much liquor."

"It was just beer, Claude."

"Beer, liquor—it's all the same. You drunk way too much of it and I dont like the way it make you act. You just stand around lookin stupid and dopey to my way of thinkin and that aint no good sign. Where you learn to drink like that? I realize it was plenty here to be drunk but you just kept snatchin cans outta that tub like beer was goin outta style."

It was early evening, almost dark, and I too felt not only picnicked out but baseballed out, firecrackered out, joked out and thoroughly exhausted. Earlier that afternoon I had taught Harold and Tinetta, a couple of Jezzy's grandchildren, how to swim, in the dirty waters of the Detroit River. I felt proud, I must say, for someone who not very long ago, before that class at school, hadnt known a jackknife from a backstroke.

Jezzy and her gang were a few hundred yards away visiting with friends theyd run into. Claude's "intelligent" new acquaintance had called up and canceled out at the last minute. We sat at a picnic table across from one another, a few scattered kids around us, playing with sparklers, flipping over cherrybombs and blockbusters that had been sneaked in from Ohio where fireworks were still legal.

"I'm not drunk," I told Claude, "I'm OK."

"No? Just the same you drink too much. I been so scared of you gettin on dope that I'd done clean overlooked the drinkin possibility."

"It's been a hot day. I needed somethin to cool me down."

"I likes to keep cool myself and this here cocola is pretty good for that too, you know. You ever try any of that, or is that outta your class now, you so grown?"

"Claude. Ive been thinking about goin away for a coupla weeks. To New York."

She didnt bat an eye. "New York, hunh? What is it that's in New York that you cant find here?"

"I'm not askin to go for a year or even for a few months—just a coupla weeks."

"For a vacation, hunh? What would you do, who do you know that live over there?"

"Billy Sanchez."

"Is that where he at now? How is he doin with his old sincere self?"

All the kids were getting quiet to watch one of the park-sponsored fireworks shows going on in the sky way over near the beautiful band shell, the illuminated amphitheater where the Detroit Symphony once assembled to broadcast summer concert favorites over WWJ.

Little Harold, age six, asked me, "How do they make em turn all those different colors after they shoot em way up in the sky, MC?"

"It's all done with chemistry."

"But how do they do it?"

"They just put different chemicals in that go off at different times after you light em, that's all I know."

"Oooo look at that one," his sister said, pointing.

"When I was a little girl, much younger than you are now, MC," Claude said, "I use to listen to Kate Smith over the radio. You dont know nothin about that. This was back down in Mississippi. She use to would come on the air and sing her little mess and talk to the people and I'd be one of em out there listenin. She was so kind and generous it seemed like to me, and I wanted to leave home so bad that I always thought to myself if I could just get to New York and find Kate Smith that all my troubles would be over, and I could live with her and she would look after me and see to it that everything was all right. Wasnt I foolish? It's hard for me to believe that I even use to think like that."

"Kate Smith, hunh?"

"Kate Smith, darlin."

We watched the fireworks display for a while.

"If I was to say OK, that you could go over here to New York for a couple weeks, what would you do with your group and your music?"

"We're breaking up, dont you know?"

"How come?"

"Everybody's goin his own way. Shakes' folks dont want him to be mixed up with the music business anymore. Jimmy's joined the service and you already know about Billy Sanchez."

"He sure had a lotta spunk for a blind boy. I always liked him, he was such a gentleman and so sincere." She took a sip of Coke and looked at her watch. "It's bout time for Jezzy and them to be getting they old late boodies back over here. It's done got dark and we got to get this stuff packed. Listen, child. I wouldnt begrudge you a two-week vacation trip to New York since it's summertime and since you have worked so hard this last year. You have earned it, I think. It just so happen I got a vacation comin up myself—three weeks, and I been thinkin bout goin back south to visit my mama and papa. They havent been doin too well and you know I havent seen them in five or six years, goin on. Maybe we can work somethin out."

"You could go south while I went east."

"That's kinda what I was thinkin. What if you was to go to New York and I was to take the train down to Meridian and we could keep in contact with one another until we got back? Then you could start to think about what school or college you wanna go to and start gettin ready."

"Mama, I sure could go for that. All I wanna do is visit a few places, walk around and see if this New York is all people make it out to be. I could stay at the Y. After all, if I'm gonna go on in music I might even end up livin there one of these days."

"I guess that's what you got your mind set on, much as I hate to admit it. It might be good for you to get outta town for a little bit. No, I wouldnt try to keep you from goin to New York, but I sure would feel better if it was somebody else goin long with you. Maybe you can find out where Billy Sanchez live when you there and spend some time with him. I even kinda wish you was goin back home with me so Mama and Papa and them could get a chance to see you, see what you look like in person. They aint seen you since you was round twelve. Ahh, you was so funny-lookin then—and now you done grown up to be such a fine-lookin young man."

ELEVEN

THAT LAST full week in Detroit was one of the strangest times of my life. I felt happy and in pain at the same time. I was happy to be getting away, but it hurt to be leaving my friends behind, the only friends I'd ever had, and Donna Lee.

"Will you think of me?" she wanted to know, her unforgettable brown eyes filled up with light. "I wanted to do something for you before you got away, something good." She gripped my hand very tightly and gazed out across the water.

We had necked thru movies at the Fisher Theater that afternoon, and afterwards, knowing nothing better to do, toured the GM Bldg., the street floor, the display room where Shakes and I went as kids to sit around in Cadillacs and pretend that we were driving until the guard would turn up and run all the unruly black kids off. "You the ones been swipin our ashtrays and hubcaps!" he always shouted. The crowd in there had been unbearable, so Donna and I had gone downtown to sit on benches along the waterfront, hoping for a breeze to soften the heat. Nuts in speedboats roared up and down the river. Donna even thought she recognized Erica Dobson on a yacht that passed by.

"Es un día muy bonito," I told her, practicing the little Spanish I knew. Donna could really speak it. She had been president of the Spanish Club.

"Yes, it is a beautiful day," she said, *"pero al fondo de mi corazón hay una tristeza, un dolor profundo, muy profundo, profundísimo, querido mío."*

"I'm sorry but youre gonna have to break that one down for me, baby."

"You mean you didnt understand that?"

"Well, the gist of it–you dont feel too good, right?"

"I said that at the bottom of my heart there's a sadness, *tristeza,* a very deep sadness in fact."

"Deepísimo, eh?"

"O, forget it, let's talk English."

"Let's talk splib."

"For somebody who's about to walk out of my life and who I'll be missing–you sure are silly."

"I'll only be gone a little while."

"You say two weeks but youre taking your guitar with you. Anything can happen."

"Like what?"

"You could find a job with a band and stay in New York, or fall off the Empire State Building, or–"

"How about the Statue of Liberty, me falling off that, wouldnt that be a trip! I'll miss you too, Donna. I'll write you letters every day."

"Will you really? Promise?"

"Promise."

"Will you write me a letter the first day you get

there and let me know how you are and what youre doing?"

"Promise."

"If you ran into Billy Sanchez, say, and he got you a job with a group—would you stay there? It would be just like you to pull something like that!"

"First of all, lady, before you can work as a musician in New York you have to establish residency and live there for quite a few months before the union'll let you work."

"But I know your music comes first."

"What makes you think that?"

"Oh, MC, dont play with me. Dont you understand—I love you and I hate to see you go. Do you think I'm being selfish?"

A flock of fat city pigeons zeroed in and landed at our feet. I said, "Hey, Ive got some change—let's put some money in the telescope and look across to Canada!"

"Who wants to look at Windsor, Ontario?"

"Have you ever been there?"

"Yes, lots of times."

"What's it like?"

"Same as here. Daddy kept saying, 'Look, you guys, we're in a foreign country,' but it all looked the same to me, except people seemed a little more small-townish. I dont wanna talk about Windsor."

"What do you wanna do?"

"I want—to be with you."

"Youre with me."

"That isnt what I mean."

I put my arm around her. "We're together now,

Donna, and we'll be together again. Soon."

"Just like it says in the song."

"Hmmm . . ."

"I want you to love me, MC."

"I do."

"Say it."

"I—I like you more than anyone I know, any girl."

"How many other girls do you know?"

"None of course."

She giggled. "Well, what if you meet some fabulous sophisticated girls in New York and forget about me?"

"Yes, and get married and live in a luxurious penthouse overlookin the New York River."

"Fool, there isnt any New York River—either the East River or the Hudson or the Atlantic Ocean."

"Youre so damn smart."

"Too smart for my own damn good. Men dont like girls who're smart."

"What makes you think that? I like you."

"You like me but you dont love me, you wont say you love me."

"I only just got to know you, Donna."

"Youve known me since the tenth grade when we both came to school from junior high."

"I knew about you then but I didnt really know you. Let's go look at Canada."

"MC. I wish we knew each other better, I wish we had time to get to know each other better."

"I wish you wouldnt talk so much, and I wish youd stop actin like I'm goin off to war. I'm only goin to New York City and New York City's just a few hundred miles from here."

"Around six hundred to be more exact."

"OK, six hundred, and an airplane can get me there in less than two hours."

"Youre taking a plane?"

Before she could start up another round, I took her hand and we started walking, looking for a spot where there werent many people.

"It's too bad you dont drive, MC, and dont have a car."

"I was just thinkin the same thing myself."

TWELVE

MORE THAN anyone else I wanted Shakes to go with me, but he wouldnt, he couldnt. His father had reestablished some strange control over him that I didnt really understand. He was on a sort of probation and would either have to toe the line at home or be ostracized, and when it came right down to it Shakes didnt seem that eager to leave home. This didnt surprise me now as much as it might have a year ago. Shakes, after all, had been brought up in a super-protective scene and wasnt as given to taking real chances as he would have had me believe. "Sure would like to make that run with you, man, but these people round here got me walkin a tightwire. My old man throws that marijuana jive up in my face every time I open my mouth. But I know you gonna dig it tho —all that music, those clubs and scenes and places, and you only got to be eighteen to get in and get a drink. I might join you later, man, I just might up and do that little thing."

"I dont know what to do, man."

"Just get on a jet and swoop, that's what you do."

"I mean, what if it should turn out I'd like to stay longer than two weeks?"

"How much bread you carryin with you?"

"I got about four hundred dollars of the bread I saved up. Claude doesn't want me to take that much, but I told her it was my money, that I'd earned it. She doesnt seem to be fightin me anymore, not like she used to anyway. It's almost like she's ready to give up on me or somethin."

"Wish my old lady and my old man'd give up on me. Where you gon be stayin when you get there?"

"Probably at the Y. I dont know."

"Well, drop me a card after you get straight and fill me in on the haps and dont be surprised if I turn up while you still there. I been thinkin bout packin my sticks and makin that trip myself. It's too bad the band had to break up like this."

"Yeah, it's a pretty cold shot all around."

"But we gettin warmer. I can feel it. We gettin warmer all the time. We gon get it together too— one of these days, after while."

"After while," I told him, shaking hands.

"Why dont you have Abdullah lay some names of people to see on you before you cut out."

"I dont wanna be hasslin any people, man."

"You might get lonesome."

"Let's just see what happens."

"Why dont you carry some copies of our jam with you too to lay on some people. Somebody might hear it and dig on it, man, and maybe you could get some new action goin for us."

"Later, Shakes."

"Later, baby."

THIRTEEN

CLAUDE KICKED up such a fuss about my going by plane that I canceled my reservation and bought a bus ticket. Air travel terrified her. She herself was going south by train. "If the train crash, maybe I could still be in good enough shape to get out and walk—but them devilish planes and jets and things, unh-unhhh, ñoooo, honey! Claude aint gon get on one. You goin *down* when one of them things crash dont care how much you wiggle and duck."

I also changed my mind about taking all my equipment. The guitar itself was enough. I could always send for the amp if necessary. I did, however, pack my journal, a few of my favorite books and three or four albums with the rest of my things. If I got lonesome, I reasoned, I could always read. Not having a portable recordplayer, the packing of the records was completely irrational. I even took Shakes' suggestion and threw a dozen or so copies of *Snakes* into the bag at the last minute. Moonbeam had stacks and stacks of them left, and Mr. Salah had gladly wrapped me a few when I went around to tell him to forget about me and the Masters of Ceremony.

"If you should change your mind," he told me coldly, "you know where you can reach us. I still think if we put our heads together we could still even now build a nice thing around you yourself —but you go on to New York, mess around, see what it's like there. Youll appreciate what I was trying to do for you guys. You might be passing up a fortune, kid."

Claude hit the number for seventy-five dollars and pushed twenty-five dollars of it into my coat pocket as I was waiting to board the bus. I didnt know what to say. I hadnt known what to say for days. She said a lot but mostly it was the same kind of thing she had always said. "You oughtta stay here over the weekend, a coupla more days, and we could go to church together like we use to do. Two more days aint gon make that much difference. New York can go on without you, dont you think?"

I put my hand on her shoulder and shook my head.

"Eat, you hear? Dont you be goin round so fascinated you forget to eat. And dont be stuffin yourself up with junk all the time. I heard how them people there eats–hotdogs and hamburgers and junk. Dont run yourself down into bad health. And try not to do anything you might be shame of later on. If you got to have anything to do with women–and I might as well tell you this cause you grown now–use some sense and get you some protection. It's a lotta bad disease goin round in a place like that."

"Claude!"

"I'm not tryna get in your business but I know young people. Believe it or not I was once young myself. I know what young people do and I think I know you. Did you have a good cry when you went in the men's room a few minutes ago?"

"What makes you think I done any cryin?"

She winked at me. "You keep forgettin I live in the world too."

The P. A. was blatting out something about Pennsylvania, New York, and my heart began to beat fast again. The baggage was loaded and most of the passengers had already boarded.

Claude hugged me hard for a long time before the flood came on. She just couldnt hold it back any longer. "O my baby, my baby, my onliest child. God bless you. Please look after yourself and try and get back here in one piece, will you . . ."

The lump in my throat was melting and hardening at the same time. I pulled away, breaking the embrace, and picked up my guitar case. "I'll phone you first thing and let you know I'm all right."

"Better step it up if you plan to make this bus,

fella!," the bus driver shouted in our direction.

"I'll be here till Wednesday and then I'm leavin for Jackson. Dont you lose Mama's and Papa's address, and write me, just send me a postcard if nothin else."

I boarded, picked a seat, the only seat left, next to a white kid who looked to be my age, a little older perhaps. He had a funny mustache and his hair was long but he seemed so much friendlier than anyone else. I settled into the aisle seat next to him and leaned to wave Claude a thousand waves. She was still standing on the concourse in her lady suit, hair freshly pressed and mouth lipsticked, all that just to see me off. Suddenly I felt very sorry for her, for her whole life, for all the time she had spent working bad jobs, years of that misery just to keep us going. For the first time I noticed how young a woman she was. My friends had mothers who were around her age. There was still something pretty about her as well; something warm that glowed from her face. She needed some man to take care of her. *I'll make it all up to you,* I promised her silently.

Even after the bus had pulled away and was headed toward Michigan Ave. to get to the highway, she was still there, in my mind, waving and wiping her eyes.

I let my seat back, took a deep breath and felt around my pockets for a Kool.

"You play guitar?" the boy next to me asked.

"Little bit."

"I do too."

"What kinda stuff?"

"Folk and rock and stuff like that, but Ive really been trying to get into some blues and jazz lately. Have you worked professionally?"

"I used to have a little band. We worked a few jobs."

"O yeah, what was the name of your group?"

"The Masters of Ceremony."

"Hmm, never heard of them. What kinds of things did you play?"

"No name for it—just music, I guess. We made up a lot of our own material—sort of a blend between rhythm and blues and jazz, I suppose you could say."

"That's interesting. Ive just finished reading a fine history of the blues that you might be interested in taking a look at sometime. It's packed in my grip but I can write the name of it down for you. I play around school with a crazy kind of group but we mostly just play fraternity jobs, you know. How far you going?"

"New York."

"O, youve got a long ride ahead of you. Why dont you fly?"

"Thought I'd take in some of the scenery. Ive never been in that part of the country before."

"It's nothing but freeway clear on thru. You going to be working there, in New York?"

"Nah, just visitin."

"First time, eh? I'd sure like to go there one day. My roommate at school's from Long Island and he's always trying to get me to come spend semester breaks and vacations with him and his family. Do you know many people there?"

"Ive got a few names."

"Well, maybe you would like a couple more. My roommate lives there, like I said. He's a nice guy but kind of weird, I know he'd like you. He likes anybody who plays guitar, especially if they know anything about blues. He isnt a bad blues player himself—country blues, you know? He's really quite good but he's always anxious to meet someone who could teach him new things. He plays most of his blues in E and A major but he's been trying to get out of that rut. Poor guy, he's really going to flunk out of school if he doesnt stop spending all of his time on guitar."

"I know the feeling."

"I'll give you his address and phone number and you can phone him after you get settled and just tell him I sent you—my name's Greg. He's spending the summer in the Village, that's a place in downtown New York where all the swingers stay. The stories he tells me! You wouldnt believe some of them. He's even been dating a colored girl—and boy, is she ever a babe, he's sent me pictures, wow!"

"Well, write his name down before you get off and also the name of that book. How far *you* goin?"

"Only as far as Cleveland. I'm almost ashamed to admit it. But it has one redeeming advantage. My dad owns a big music store there which is nice because I can get discounts on guitars and banjos for all my friends."

The miles flew by and soon it was night. It grew chilly and I missed my nice warm room at home.

The college boy talked himself down and fell

asleep. I rented a pillow at one of the stops, let my seat all the way back but couldnt even so much as nap, so I sat up straight again and wrote letters to Donna Lee in my head; letters to Donna Lee and letters to Claude.

Also, I tried to write my diary entry for the day in my head but could only get as far as saying: *For the first time in my life I don't feel trapped; I don't feel free either but I don't feel trapped & I'm going to try & make this feeling last for as long as I can*

I smoked another cigarette and wondered what I was doing.

THE LAUREL SERIES OF GREAT SHORT STORIES